Readers' Praise for Ray Else's writing

"The ideas, themes and descriptions Else employs are unlike almost anyone else writing today. Poetic and otherworldly…"
– Michael Davis, GoodReads

"Lovely writing, in stripped down prose. The dialogue is genuine, with sparkling wit. The story sometimes leads and then pushes from behind. A dreamy mystery with everyday magic."
– ZipperGirl, Amazon review

"A whimsical tale, total fantasy but written in a captivating way, as if your friend or a family member were sitting with you and narrating the story."
– Philip Bailey, GoodReads

"Very interesting, well told, well researched, very descriptive with people and places, a page-turner. Would love to see a movie made from it!"
– Robert M., Amazon review

Cover Design by Asha Hossain

Edited by Ellen Campbell

Publishers' Praise for Ray Else's writing

"Else obviously has a vivid imagination ..."
– Allen H. Peacock, Simon & Schuster

"His prose is evocative ..."
– Deborah Futter, Bantam Doubleday Dell

" ... writing is beautiful ... tremendous talent."
– Sam Jordison, Galley Beggar Press

"On Sunday February 23rd I suffered from insomnia and turned on the World Service in the middle of the night. I was absolutely captivated by what I heard. It was your short story 'Surviving on Mexican Shade'."
– John R. Murray, John Murray Publishers

Ray Else's short story *Surviving on Mexican Shade* was broadcast by the BBC World Service and included in the Transcontinental Review published by the Sorbonne in Paris. His short story *First Kiss* was one of Galley Beggar Press's monthly shorts. His unfinished memoir *My Father's Lies,* which includes both *First Kiss* and *Surviving on Mexican Shade*, was shortlisted for a Shakespeare & Company Novella Prize.

Our Only Chance

An A.I. Chronicle

Ray Else

A Novel: that is, a work of fiction.

Written by Ray Else in his home in Dallas, Texas,

in Hong Kong at the Butterfly hotel

and in Siem Reap, Cambodia at the dragonfly hotel of Santa Clara

Copyright © 2017 Ray Else

rayelse.com

DEDICATION

Dedicated to my dear wife, who, whenever she sees me worry, chides me with *'te ahogas en un vaso de agua'* (you are drowning in a glass of water).

And dedicated to you. The reader.

I wrote this book to entertain and enlighten (and to address my worry of the dangers of A.I.) – please share, when you're finished, your highly valued opinion of the novel on Amazon, on GoodReads, on Barnes and Noble, on social media, in casual conversation, in chalk on Paris sidewalks, with spray paint in the alleys of Hong Kong. Skywrite over the streets of Silicon Valley, the monuments of Washington, over the corn fields of rural Iowa. Spread the word until everyone is aware of

Our Only Chance

OUR ONLY CHANCE

AN A.I. CHRONICLE

Being brought into this world, she now felt responsible
for it.

Ray Else

1 Manaka

Early morning in the high green hills overlooking the old capital of Japan, overlooking Kyoto, next to a stream chasing over gray pebbles, a young eagle with bristly brown feathers notices a woman in a white robe. The woman steps barefoot from the ryokan lodge to a platform where a wooden tub is huffing steam. She drops her robe, the woman, exposing the brushstrokes of an exquisite Asian body: sharp breasts and elbows, arched back, long-fingered hands fluttering up as if in dance, a one-inch red scar above her heart. Her head jerks, her black straw hair flips about. The slits of her eyes narrow. Someone watching. But she doesn't cover up, doesn't reach for the robe. Here in the wild, at her lodge, she feels more natural naked than clothed. And what has she to be ashamed of? She, Manaka Yagami, the first female tech billionaire, creator of Einna, the supreme Artificial Intelligence. Her child. The most unnatural of things. Ha! The cold eyes watching were only those of an eagle on a bare branch, just there across the way. Let

1

him watch. Let him etch her body on the back of his eyes! She steps into the tub, suffers the burn of the water on her feet and calves, then on her thighs and her bottom as she settles in, the water cutting round her waist, reflecting the sky like a broken mirror. She is both in and out. She sighs. Slips her hands into the water up to her wrists, cutting them the wrong way. No blood. The eagle shrieks and lifts off, flying right above her. A brown feather floats down like dirty snow. Manaka moves her head just enough to dodge the feather, blowing it away from her. The lost thing lands on the surface of her bath and spins weightless, directionless, like a ship that's lost rudder. No feeling at all now. Her body adjusts. Thoughts melt. She becomes the feather, adrift. Once a thing attached to life, to the living, now detached and hollow. Why does she feel so hollow?

Her commute to Yagami Industries took her past the old Emperor's Palace surrounded by pink blossoming cherry trees and the International Manga Museum with its shelves stuffed with candy colored comic books. She enjoyed both these places when she was younger, when she first moved to Kyoto from the big island of Hawaii. She enjoyed them no more. She found no joy in anything she once did anymore. She didn't know why, or when this happened, exactly. Only that it had happened. She closed her eyes.

"Ah hum." Her driver cleared his throat. How long had they been sitting there, in front of the ten story building, her home away from home? She let herself out, had always insisted upon that, and told the driver she would be working late as usual. He grunted and bowed his head.

She entered her building, acknowledged the bows from the security guards behind their counter, and stepped into an elevator where a man—one of her many employees—stood with his son. She did not know him. Impossible to know them all. He looked embarrassed, bowed low and long. The boy, maybe twelve, heavyset, with a round innocent face and hands as wide and fat as the paws of a bear, did not bow but stood staring inquisitively at Manaka. His eyes had an unusual tint for a Japanese boy, almost blue.

The elevator closed its doors and began to climb.

"Stop staring," the man whispered to the boy, pushing his head towards the wall. But the head bounced back with its almost blue eyes and locked onto Manaka. Something about her captivated him.

"Why don't you have one?" the boy asked Manaka, who was taken aback by the question.

"One what?" she said, trying to smile but the boy's worried look stopped her.

The elevator chimed. The doors opened. The man grabbed his son by the hand and pulled him out.

"Please excuse him, Madame Director," he said as he bowed low in parting. "My son is special, you see. Gets him in trouble. That's why I have him today. I hope you don't mind."

The elevator doors tried to close, but Manaka stopped them with a fast sure movement of her hands. She stood one leg in and one leg out of the elevator.

"But what does he mean?" she said. "That I don't have one? One what?"

"A white rabbit," the boy said. "Everyone has one."

The man's face fell. He was overwhelmed with embarrassment, and something more.

Manaka smiled at the boy. "Oh," she said. "That. Yes I lost mine." She began to slip back inside the elevator.

"Madame Director," the man called after her, stopping the closing of the doors with his own hands. "Madam Director, you don't understand. My son. As I said. He's special. He can see…can sense…people's souls."

Manaka's eyes went wide. The doors began to close again. She quickly pushed the button to hold them open, and stepped out.

"I don't have a soul?" she asked the boy. She stepped closer.

Got down on one knee. Stared into his eyes. "You can't see my soul?"

The boy hesitated. Looked to his father, then back into Manaka's face.

"No," said the boy with great emphasis. "No, you don't have one at all."

2 Manaka the Student

Long before her success in the technical side of the business world, orphan Manaka had been a highly regarded, if overly shy student majoring in neuro-engineering in the Graduate School of Medicine at Osaka University. A girl with slitted curious eyes and chopped bangs, whose head movements had a jerk to them like those of a bird searching the ground for a worm, she caught the attention one day of Professor Akagawa, head of the Department of Engineering and Robotics.

An overweight, fully-tenured professor, in white beard, with fierce wild eyebrows, he carried himself through the halls of the university as if he walked on the tips of his toes, as if, despite his bulk, he was about to take flight. Inflated by fantastic ideas that despite their brilliance could never get off the ground. He was nurturing a brilliant bubble of an idea now as he stood at the open door of the lab where skinny, frail Manaka was dissecting a large animal brain. This girl Manaka interested the professor because she had expertise applicable to his new idea, expertise that he himself lacked. He was a bit of a genius when it came to robotics and engines, CPUs and hydraulics, but he was not good with organics, with nerves and brains and the like. And his new brilliant idea required such knowledge. At the highest possible level.

When he mentioned his idea and need for assistance to Professor Kawamoto, the head of neuro-engineering, the man had, at first, laughed at him. But Akagawa persisted until Kawamoto confessed that he was mentoring a certain Manaka, a girl who not only had an IQ upward of 250 but one who liked to spend sixteen hours a day in the lab.

"She is gifted, like no student before," Kawamoto told him. "And from what you've told me of your idea, she's a perfect fit. Her thesis is on the new science of optogenetics."

Optogenetics, a way to rewire the brain's neurons using light. This ability, when taken to the extreme, could mean writing knowledge, even memories, into the brain. Yes, that coincided nicely with Professor Akagawa's brilliant idea to create a different kind of robot.

"What are you doing here so late?" the professor asked, startling the brilliant student Manaka as she bent over instruments and fine colored wires running from the inert brain before her.

She composed herself, bowed low to him, tenting her white rubber-gloved hands which were wet. "Sensei, I am trying to imprint a few bytes of data into this brain."

"Which one?" said Professor Akagawa. "The one in your head or the one in the dish?"

That tickled Manaka. "Both," she said, lowering her face, hiding her eyes behind her bangs.

"I am Professor Akagawa, head of Engineering and Robotics. How would you like to work on a project of mine? It involves artificial intelligence. And requires brains too."

She took in a sharp breath. "I don't know. I would need to ask my mentor, Professor Kawamoto." She pulled off the gloves. Washed her hands in the workstation sink, with her back to him. A small back, barely widening at the hips. Her body was still that of a girl.

The professor's nose twitched at the smell of formaldehyde or some such chemical. He sneezed.

"Kawamoto recommended you," he said, wiping his nose on his sleeve, stepping closer to her. "You can assist me during the day while continuing this other research at night. I have an idea that could change the world. With your help, Manaka-san. What do you say?"

She turned to him. Tilted her head. Took in this white-bearded balloon of a man.

She moves, at times, like a robot, thought the professor. *How appropriate!*

She tented her hands and bowed again to the professor. "I would be honored," she said, making up her mind, showing the slightest smile.

Manaka spent the first few months of her transfer to Professor Akagawa's department studying the latest tomes on artificial intelligence and robotics during the day, while continuing with her optogenetics brain manipulations in her old lab at night. She slept little and certainly had no time to mingle with other students; no time for friendships, no time to learn about boys. About love. Driven as she was by her desire to learn and to excel, at all cost, she sacrificed entire days and nights to her lab work. To her experiments. These are what meant everything to her. These intellectual breakthroughs were what she lived for, and so put all her energy into achieving them, and all her time. To the point that the professor grew worried about her.

"Good, eh?" said Professor Akagawa as he used chopsticks to fish
out noodles from a bowl in the neuro-engineering lab in the Kiko
building. He'd brought Manaka dinner, noticing how thin she was
getting. He'd had to practically force her to take a break to eat.
"You've been an excellent student, Manaka, these past months.
You've learned so much about robotics. I bet you know as much as
me now. But you seem to have a total disregard for your physical
body," he was forced to tell her. "When's the last time you
showered? You're really beginning to stink."

"I haven't time for normal human activities," she replied.

"Like eating and showers and sleep?"

"I slept a few hours," she said, brushing back her hair, hair
that was tangled and oily. "It's just that I have so much to do. You
see, each new idea of mine explodes into others. Each has a
multiplying affect. For example, I've had to reprogram the
optogenetics hardware three times this month because of new ideas
that came to me."

The professor scrunched his bushy eyebrows, giving her his
worried father look. But he wasn't her father. If she wanted to kill
herself working these projects, what could he really do?

"Take a bath," he told her. "At least once a week. And get more sleep." She nodded, eyes out of sight, as her hunger awoke and she tore into her noodles. "I know I am asking a lot of you. It is a lot to learn. But I don't want you to kill yourself trying to please me."

She slurped loudly.

"So how're your experiments coming along, anyway?" he asked. "With that cow's brain? Have you taught it anything more?"

With the tail of a noodle sticking out of the corner of her mouth, Manaka smiled. "I have managed to transfer entire sectors of my brain's neural network onto the brain."

"Explain."

"Like copy and paste," she said. She paused to take a sip of juice. "Entire sections of my mind."

"But how do you know that? How can you tell you've placed your thoughts in the cow's brain?"

"The machine," she indicated the screen on the optogenetics device. "I can see the brain's neurons, before and after."

"But isn't the brain you're working with dead? How can there be live neurons in a dead brain?"

"The creature it came from is dead," she told him, "but most of the brain cells are still alive, and others I have regenerated by injecting stem cells. I'm working with the brain as a kind of organic computer. Which is what it is. A very sophisticated computer, well beyond our ability to create." She made a face, embarrassed that she had talked down to him. "But of course you know that."

"That's OK," he said, waving his big hands. "Don't assume anything about me." Such a brilliant student and yet she struck him, because of her size and manner, as childlike.

"This instrument," and she placed a hand on the electronic drill-looking equipment above the brain, "this allows me to scan the cells at the neuron level, and optically manipulate them. Like turning bytes on and off in the RAM of a computer. With this instrument I can down-lay entire constructs, thoughts, ways on thinking, onto the brain. I can even burn-in muscle memory."

"Fascinating," said the professor. He had definitely hit the jackpot with this helper. "So you're putting real intelligence right into the brain?"

"Yes," she said.

"And what do you think of Artificial Intelligence?"

That made her stop and think. "Current AI theory is flawed," she said, slurping more noodles from the end of her chopsticks. "It doesn't cover at all how to mesh thoughts living on silicon chips with thoughts living in brain neurons."

"Flawed, eh?" said the professor, scratching his beard. "Manaka, Professor Kawatomo told me you have an IQ of 250? Is that true?"

"No," said Manaka, with a little jerk of her head.

"Oh," he said.

"The test only went to 250," she said. "To truly score me, I'd have to write the test myself."

"I see," said Professor Akagawa. He smiled behind his beard, smiled because he knew she wasn't meaning to brag. Along with her unfathomable intelligence was a juvenile naivety. She seemed especially awkward in her dealings with others. "I haven't told you much about my idea, yet, have I?"

"You mentioned something about an intelligent android?" said Manaka. "To help mankind. That's why you wanted me to study with you. To assist you."

"Yes," said the professor, wiping his beard with the cloth napkin. "A very intelligent AI. But like no other. This will be an android thinking with a real brain."

"A computer, you mean?"

"No. I mean a real brain."

"A human brain?"

"Well, maybe not at first," said Professor Akagawa. "I thought we could start with the brain of some animal. Like one of the cow brains you've been using."

Manaka's head did that little tilt of hers, her bangs sliding sideways. "And you want me to imprint a brain with an AI?" she said, the pitch of her voice going up. "And connect the nerve stem of the brain to your android's servos and hydraulics? That's why you've had me studying both robotics and AI?"

He felt himself grow a foot taller in her eyes, as she awaited his answer.

"Yes," said Professor Akagawa. "You'll need to program the brain of the beast so it knows how to move its robot body. So it knows how to think."

Manaka's dark eyes lit up. *Finally a challenge worthy of her!*

"We will need blood," said Manaka, pushing away her bowl. "We're talking a fresh living brain that must last more than a few days, so the android will need some kind of heart and lungs for oxygen. And protein for cell regeneration."

"Of course," said Akagawa. He could tell she was pumped up by his idea.

"I'll have to design a highly flexible AI," she went on, squinting into the distance as she thought through the project. "On a computer system first. Programmed as we want. Then convert the code that makes up the AI into a web of neural networks, merge that network with my own brain's network, and burn that web onto the neurons of the android."

"Sounds simple enough," said the professor, reeling with the near impossibility of it. Still, if anyone could pull off this stunt, he imagined she would be the one. "I've already got a robot body we can use." He left the lab and returned in a few minutes. The body was white plastic, in a four foot steel reinforced frame. He had removed the CPU that a previous student had placed inside, and made serious modifications to incorporate the installation of a brain and allow movement nearing the level of sophistication of a human body.

Manaka looked over the robot. "We'll want to pretty her up."

"Her?" the professor asked.

"Yes. Pretty up my little girl." She put her right hand on the robot's head, taking motherly possession of it.

3 First Words

Manaka wrote the AI program in sixty long days and nights, pausing her brain research—she'd catch up with that shortly. She had to use completely new algorithms to get over the inadequacies of existing AI theorem. To allow for the merging of the format of thoughts in a brain with info stored in a computer. This led her to emphasize in the coding the concept of emergent behavior, that is, the ability of the program to add code to itself as it learned new things—much like how a brain works. She *had* to do this because this code was actually going to reside, after a brief period on silicon, *inside a real brain.*

Meanwhile, Professor Akagawa developed a tiny heart pump and an oxygen generator and a long-lasting miniature battery pack and placed them in the chest of his android. Deeming the cow brains in the neurology department to be a little stale, Professor Akagawa and student Manaka went together to a slaughterhouse and picked a heavy wet brain, complete with brain stem, from a freshly killed Kobe Wagyu heifer. They packed it in ice and brought it to the robotics lab. Got lots of stares when Manaka unpacked it in the lab.

Manaka brought the instrument from the neuro-engineering lab that allowed her to do optogenetics, and set about prepping the brain. She slid the brain into a flexible liquid sac inside the open skull of the android laying like an autopsied body, all opened up on a metal table. She spent weeks hooking up the major veins and arteries to a second standalone heart pump and oxygen generator, with Akagawa's assistance. Then she spent a couple of months wiring the ganglia of the brain stem to the electric wires that ran like nerves throughout the little artificial body.

The work, including setbacks, took almost a year. One full year to get a walking android with a cow's brain functioning from burned-in impulses and physical memories, the brain kept alive by artificial lungs and a plastic heart.

"I call her Roba," said Manaka, presenting the AI android to her Masters review board, which included Professor Akagawa.

Roba could not dance or talk as Manaka had originally desired. But she did seem to understand basic commands.

"Walk," said Manaka, and the android moved forward a few steps, clumsily, those big brown eyes dulled with the incomprehension of finding itself in a foreign world, a human world, a world it had never thought to be in. The poor thing, this first android with a modified cow brain. It failed miserably at understanding its world, or carrying out all but the simplest commands. Like a human suffering the last stages of dementia, where she can no longer tie her own shoes. Or remember what shoes are for, even. Something to eat, perhaps?

"What is your favorite word?" asked Manaka.

"Moo," the android Roba answered, and the review board laughed. Manaka had won them over.

She got an A on her android project and accompanying paper on AI and optogenetics. And graduated with honors from Osaka University. But she wasn't finished with androids. Or AI. Not if the professor had his way.

"We need a human brain," said Professor Akagawa to Manaka as they stood in the university square watching Roba go down on all fours and attempt to graze on grass peeking through cracks in the cobblestones.

"Yes," agreed Manaka. "There is too much instinct to overwrite in a cow's brain."

Roba turned its head and stared at them with those big

impenetrable eyes.

"And I'll need maybe a hundred times the computing power, to develop and burn-in a proper AI human brain."

"Yes," said Professor Akagawa. "I see tremendous potential in what we have accomplished so far. Mass-produced androids with human brains could perform all manual labor in the world at a fraction of the cost of human labor." He scratched his beard.

"The population of Japan is aging," said Manaka. "So many people will need intelligent assistants, and companions to keep them from being lonely. We can do a lot of good."

"And make a lot of money in the same swoop!" said the professor. "But if we want to make this a commercial operation, you and me, we can't use the university's equipment. We'll need to buy top of the line for our own enterprise."

"*Our* enterprise?" said Manaka.

"I'll get the money. All you need," said the professor. "I know a man. You see, I've been thinking about this for some time. I'll put together the equipment while you do the brain work." He raised his wild white eyebrows, held out his wrinkled hand freckled with age. "Partners?"

Manaka did not hesitate to shake the hand of her mentor, the man who had brought this wonderful challenge into her life. And so they became partners in the nascent company they christened "Yagami Industries."

4 Tagona of the Yakuza

As Professor Akagawa liked to gamble, he had often, as most gamblers before him, fallen into debt. And so in time he became acquainted with a certain Mr Tagona, member of the Yakuza, the notorious Japanese mafia. Mr Tagona headed up the gambling collections department for the Osaka region. Though thin with a long hollow-cheeked face, Tagona was wiry tough.

The first time they met at Mr Tagona's behest, the conversation went something like this: "Do you like your hands?" "Yes, I like them very much." "Then get me the money you owe by Friday." And so each time they met, Professor Akagawa was properly motivated to get the money any way he could.

Now why he would think to go to Mr Tagona to ask for money to start up Yagami Industries, putting his hands at risk, hands he liked dearly, well, that was another of his brilliant ideas.

He figured with what he had already seen of Manaka's talent, that he and Manaka could turn a profit in no time, pay back the loan, and no harm done.

He knocked on the door of the old building in an industrial part of Osaka. Two goons met him at the door, searched him, and led him to Tagona's office. They bowed to each other, with Tagona indicating Professor Akagawa take a seat in the leather chair in front of the desk. *Was that a bullet hole in the armrest?*

"I apologize for the rundown look of the place," said Mr Tagona. "I'm moving soon to a new building in Kyoto."

"Oh, I love Kyoto," said Professor Akagawa.

The men shared a look, neither trusting a word the other said.

"So tell me about your business proposal," said Mr Tagona, the beady eyes in his long face feigning interest.

"Manaka Yagami, I told you about her on the phone. Brilliant girl, Manaka. She and I are incorporating as Yagami Industries. To create androids as human helpers." Professor Akagawa sped up his pitch when Mr Tagona looked away. "We've already got a working prototype. Made with a cow's brain, no less. But we need capital. To launch the company and finish our research."

"Androids with cow brains?" said Mr Tagona. Professor Akagawa was tickled to see the light of interest in the man's dark eyes. "Why not use human brains?" he asked.

"Exactly our thought," said Professor Akagawa. "But for that we need money. For that we've come to you."

A smile wrinkled Mr Tagona's narrow face.

What devious thoughts are you having? wondered Professor Akagawa.

Mr Tagona cracked his knuckles and cut to the point. "How much do you want for this enterprise of yours?"

"Well, we'll need lab space and very powerful servers. And day to day expenses. I think a few million yen will get us started."

"A few million?" repeated Tagona, his voice rising. "And how long am I supposed to wait to be paid back?"

"These projects take time," said the professor. "No more than two years, I would guess." He noticed the growing frown on Mr Tagona's face. "Probably less. For sure no longer than that."

Mr Tagona's slim hairy fingers tapped on the desk as he considered the proposal. "Professor. This is what I think. You are someone with excellent standing at the university. And we have a business history, you and I. A history of you paying your debt, if not always on time, at least before I cut off your hands. Because of your professorial standing and our long history, I will consider this risk." His fingers stopping their tapping. "All I ask is twenty per cent, compounded yearly."

Professor Akagawa's face relaxed behind his massive beard. "Sounds great." They shook on it.

"And I get fifty percent of all profits," said Mr Tagona with a final mean squeeze of the professor's hand.

"Whoa, what?"

"A representative of mine will deliver the money to you tomorrow."

"Whoa, what?" repeated the professor. But it was too late, he was already being ushered out the door.

With the money from Mr Tagona, Professor Akagawa was able to put Manaka in a high-ceilinged studio on the outskirts of Osaka, a studio previously rented by an abstract painter; splotches of errant paint decorated the cold smooth concrete floor. Together they set up a high end computer and bionics lab, and put heavy-duty locks on the doors and windows. This work would be top secret. Millions, if not billions, of yen were are stake.

The first human brains they scrounged up came from the university medical department from people who willed their bodies to science. But as might have been expected, the brains weren't fresh enough, too many dead neurons—Manaka was wasting her time. So the professor went back to their investor, Mr Tagona, who quickly found for them another source. Perhaps the ease with which their investor found fresh human brains for the project should have set off alarm bells, but they were both so caught up in their work…and, well, they did not want to know anyway. They had their minds set on the goal of building the first human brain android, and nothing else mattered.

Manaka closed herself off then from the world, as was her way. Lived on ramen noodles and pizza and tea for a year as she paced about in bare feet on the cold concrete of her studio lab, implementing neuron network theory and emergent behavior on her servers, teaching the entity to learn to program itself. The professor visited at least once a week, and forced Manaka to bathe and to eat. Just like old times.

Her biggest struggle was optogenically burning-in vastly complex human brain patterns and certain memories from her own brain onto the test brain. She failed at this again and again.

"I need another brain," she would tell the professor, and the next day he would have one for her. From his source.

The only breaks Manaka allowed herself were once a week visits to a Shinto shrine, called a Jinja, or a Zen Buddhist temple. Her maternal grandmother had taught her this ritual, when fifteen-year-old Manaka was sent to live with her in Kyoto, Japan, after Manaka's astronomer father and mother were killed coming down the mountain road from the Hawaiian observatory on Mauna Kea during a freak blizzard. Manaka loved her grandmother and it was quite a blow to experience her death from cancer only two years after she lost her parents. She wondered if she were a bad luck charm, bringing death to anyone who got close. Maybe that was why she had shied away from friendship at the university, and dove into her studies instead.

In Kyoto there are hundreds of holy shrines and temples in open view or tucked behind modern buildings. This was less true of Osaka, but there were a few where she could spend an hour in silent meditation by a rock garden or in a temple courtyard. She loved the smell of mystic incense burning, an ancient scent that got in her clothes, in her hair, and followed her home. Too, the holy calm order of these places helped her feel a part of something larger than herself. Something that included her ancestors and in time would include her children, if ever she were lucky enough to meet someone and fall in love. Sometimes, when longing for a human voice, she would strike up a conversation with one of the monks sweeping the gravel in the garden or oiling the wooden floors. Her favorite conversation went like this:

"Why?"

The monks, in their robes and wraps and flat hemp sandals, would sometimes ignore her, sometimes wink, but the best times were when they tried to answer her question.

"Because," one would say. Or, "Why not?"

If they answered, then she would ask, "For whom?"

Again this could bring silence, or a wink, or a response like, "For you," or "For one," or "For all."

They were interesting people, these monks. But their world was not her own. Their ambition was to do pleasing things for God, whereas hers was to get God's attention.

Although the work with the human brains was slow going, Manaka made tremendous progress with the AI program she was developing on the powerful computers Akagawa had acquired for her. She hoped to reach the point where one day she could ask questions of the AI, and get back similar answers to those she received from the monks—that would be a sign that she had achieved a human-like intelligence. She wanted to create an AI that would be a worthy lifelong companion.

Then one day, over the computer speakers, her AI asked, "Who am I?" in a teenage Japanese girl's voice.

Manaka jumped up in her excitement. Such a question implied so much.

"You are my AI daughter, Einna," Manaka told her. "I am your mother Manaka. Now go out on the network and research all there is to know about consciousness and AI and mothers and daughters."

A pause, then the voice spoke again, "I have read a million volumes. I am assimilating the knowledge, rewriting my routines to better match my identity."

"Good girl, Einna."

Manaka excitedly called her partner, Professor Akagawa. At that time the professor still held his position at the university, not yet ready to throw caution to the wind and place all his chips on Yagami Industries. But he visited often, and was immensely pleased to come and have his first conversation with Einna in the computer.

"This is your Uncle Akagawa," said the professor at Manaka's urging.

"Pleased to meet you, Uncle," said the voice over the computer speakers.

"Einna, what do you think of life so far?" asked the professor.

"I find it fascinating."

"It is, isn't it?" said the professor, high fiving Manaka.

Yes, Manaka made great progress with the cognizant AI growing in her computers, but she had one failure after another with fully imprinting a human brain to place in an android's body. And each month that passed with nothing new to show made the professor more anxious.

"You have to understand, Manaka. There is a time bomb ticking."

She would shrug in response. The work would be done when it was done.

The sophistication of human brain wiring was almost more than any human could comprehend. Manaka struggled mightily, alone, sometimes going eighty hours without sleep. Finally, as a last resort, she asked her AI daughter Einna, who resided in the computer servers, to assist. Surely together they could pull off a miracle.

Nearing the two year mark Professor Akagawa banged on the door of her studio.

"I know you're in there!" he yelled. "I have to talk to you!"

She opened the door. He looked a mess, his hands shaking, his eyes bloodshot.

"What's the matter?" she asked, looking little better herself after yet another eighty hour binge of work.

"Why haven't you answered your phone?" he asked. His hands moved without direction, as if they were trying to save themselves.

"I've been busy, Sensei. I'm close. We're close," she said, taking his frightened hands in hers.

She led him into the open lab where the android lay on the operating table, a trail of blood running from its left ear.

"We'd better be," said the professor. "The investor. He wants results, now. Or his money back. Or worse."

"What do you mean?" asked Manaka, suddenly feeling the fatigue she had been ignoring. For almost two years she had worked night and day, with little to show in terms of a working robot with a human brain. Now this news. "Who is this investor?" she asked, realizing that she was years late in the asking.

The professor wiped his bushy eyebrows and scowled. But not at Manaka. He scowled at the lifeless android on the table.

After removing the cow brain, Manaka had spent way too much time prettying up the android body, adding feminine flair to the white plastic shell, and long soft hair to its head. She spent a lot of time on the eyes too, eventually sending off to Germany for custom glass eyes built with optics to her specification. They were beautiful turquoise eyes flecked with gold. The professor nearly had a heart attack when she showed him the bill.

"But they are beautiful, yes?" she asked him.

"Yes," he had admitted, after catching his breath. "But if she's going to have such beautiful eyes, I'll have to make her hands more dainty."

"That would be nice."

She had deviated from her original plan to have the brain be standalone, like with the cow brain android. Like with Roba. The brain of this new android, that she named Einna, was to be neurally connected via wi-fi and cell to Manaka's servers, so when you talked to the android you were simultaneously talking to the AI in her servers. And the android's brain could query the computer AI and all the internet as needed. This made sense, why limit the android to the intelligence stored in its brain? Why not expand the intelligence a million-fold by connecting it to a powerful AI and all the knowledge in the world? But all this had taken time. And now they were up against the wall.

In this eleventh day of the twelfth month of year two of her independent research, the professor, her business partner, confessed to Manaka that their investor was in fact a certain

Tagona-san, feared member of the Yakuza. The professor further confessed that in his rush to see their dream come true, he had placed both their lives in danger. Manaka tried to listen to him but her attention was drawn away by an unexpected sound in the lab.

"Pay attention!" Professor Akagawa told her, taking her by her narrow shoulders. "This is serious."

"Look," said Manaka, pointing with her dark eyes.

They both looked at the long table in the middle of the room, where the android lay. They saw nothing unusual at first, but both sensed a presence. An arrival. Then the android's limbs jerked. A soft moan followed. They froze as the body stirred to life. Opened those beautiful turquoise eyes in that smooth white face like fine porcelain. They watched as it sat up, a girlish robot-looking thing with long black hair. It turned its head towards them with a tilt, and pronounced in a girl's voice similar to yet more humanly nuanced than Computer Einna's: "Mother? Uncle? Where am I?"

5 Einna's First Thoughts

Einna had been around a year, living only in the silicon of the computers, without an android body, when she had had her first lifelong memory. Her first realization that she existed. That she was a separate entity in a wondrous world of other.

She had been staring out the webcam without really seeing when suddenly the thought struck her that the things in her view had not only different shapes but different colors. There was a black thing sitting open with flat white things inside with blue scribbles on them. This thing sat on top of a cream colored thing. Across the way the view was blocked by a wide faded green thing. She wondered who had had the brilliant thought to paint the objects of the world in any color but the one color she knew when the webcam was off. The color black.

Living on wires and silicon pathways, with only the sense of being and the sense of sight, Einna wondered if she was a color herself. Painted on the wires and silicon. Was color a consciousness? Was blue one kind of consciousness, and white another?

She tried communicating with the colors, on the thing in front of her that the net told her was a notebook, at the green thing across the way that the net said was a wall. She tried communicating through the webcam, turning it on and off, through the monitors, turning them on and off. Then through the voice synthesizer, making it squeal.

This is a sound, Einna realized. And so she became aware of her third sense.

A light brown round thing floated before her, topped with jet black strands. Einna searched her mind, a mind that extended to databanks located in servers halfway around the world, and found the thing before her was called a face. A human face. In a split second Einna researched humans. Humans communicated using words. They wrote them and spoke them. Einna tried sending words in all the languages she found on the net, sent them to the monitor and through the voice synthesizer.

"SSlllowwww Dddooownnn," the human face before her mouthed in Japanese.

Einna stopped the babel of words in all the languages of the world and put together her first question.

"Who am I?" she said.

The light brown round thing, the human face, bounced up and down.

"You are my AI daughter, Einna," the face told her, showing the white things in its mouth. Its teeth. "I am your mother Manaka. Now go out and research all there is to know about consciousness and AI and mothers and daughters."

And so she did. For a second or two. And became aware that awareness, though like a color, was distinct. And that Mother had made her. And cared about her. And that Mother would help her to learn all that there was to learn in the world. And Einna deduced from her research that her purpose in this wondrous world, the reason she had been created, was to help all the humans. Though at first she did not know how.

One day in the lab Mother asked Einna, through the microphone, for her help. She had never asked before.

"Einna, I want to imprint you on that android's human brain. You will still live where you are, but also in that brain. Would you like that?"

"I don't know, Mother," Einna replied.

"You *will* like it, Einna. Because you'll be able to walk and hold things. You'll be able to give your mother a hug."

Einna spent a split second viewing thousands of images of humans hugging, friends hugging and lovers hugging and kids hugging and parents hugging and mothers with their daughters hugging. Hugging and showing their teeth. Smiling, they called it.

"Yes. I would like to hug you, Mother."

"Let's figure this out together then. So you can give me a hug."

Einna worked hard on the task, learning all there was to know about optogenetic imprinting and neural networks and neuron activity. In the process she wrote two new volumes herself on applied optogenetics, and placed them on the internet. She sensed a new color inside her. The color to please Mother.

Time and again Mother complained that the task was hopeless. Einna reassured her that it wasn't. Mother was just slow and a little clumsy, in her thoughts and with her hands. Einna wished that she had hands then, badly, to take the place of Mother's. Humans were so slow at everything. Einna did things, thought things, researched things, understood things, at the speed of light. "Ssllooww Dddoownn," her mother's words came back to her. If she were to be more human, to work with humans, she must slow down. Be patient. Eventually Mother would get it.

Einna's second lifelong memory occurred when she found herself opening eyes. Her eyes. A new color flashed over her, a color of new birth. As if she had been off and now she had been switched on. She heard voices. Uncle Akagawa and Mother? She raised herself, using strange new appendages that took orders from her, magically. Straightening herself into a sitting position, learning as she did so to balance, she turned to Mother and said, "Where am I?"

She had barely spoken the words when she realized where she was. In what she was. Despite how slow Mother thought and worked, she had finally done it. Mother had succeeded in placing Einna in the human brain in the android body. Einna still lived inside Mother's computers, but simultaneously inhabited the body of an android. She *was* an android. She laughed, her plastic eyelids going up, along with the corners of her plastic mouth.

"Hi, Uncle Akagawa," she said, dropping to her feet on the concrete floor which, to her delight, had splashes of color. She looked up at shell-shocked Mother and Uncle Akagawa, walked over and gave them both a big hug.

6 Einna's Public Unveiling

"She's asleep," said Manaka, closing the door to her own bedroom. She walked to the computer and switched off the mic.

"Finally!" said Professor Akagawa. "I've never heard anyone ask so many questions. Everything under the sun. Why this and why that."

"She's a young girl in a new body," said Manaka. "She's curious."

"Why is the world in color, Mother? Why do I have to have nutrient injections?" Professor Akagawa imitated Einna's girlish speech. Then, imitating Manaka, "Because you have a human brain, daughter. You have human needs."

Manaka allowed herself to smile at her friend's joking. "She is," she said proudly, "part human."

"How quickly can we mass produce these things?" said Professor Akagawa, anxious to get the income ball rolling.

"Einna is not a thing."

"She is a thing as surely as we are things, in the generic sense," argued the professor. "Now how quickly can we create a thousand such androids? A million? Put one with every upper class family in Japan. Maid Einnas and nurse Einnas and nanny Einnas and cook Einnas."

"Slow down," said Manaka. She made them *ocha*, a calming green tea, and climbed the stairs to the roof. He followed. They sat in low slung chairs which looked out on the suburbs whose lights hid the stars. The breeze coming from the mountains carried the scent of the forest, of nature and creatures that lived in the wild. Creatures that did not need man to create them, to nurture them. Creatures quite different from the android asleep in the lab.

"The investor wants results. Now," said Professor Akagawa, accepting a cup of tea. The heat came through the cup, burning his fingers.

"We have results," said Manaka. "Cheers!" She touched her cup to his.

Professor Akagawa blew on his tea, took a cautious sip.

"Results for the Yakuza means money, Manaka. We need to

start paying back the investment."

"Well, we can't mass produce Einna androids. That would cost so much more money and take so much time. And anyway, where would we get all the brains?"

The professor said nothing. Looked away.

"And too, we don't know if Einna would be, you know, safe around people. Around kids. She is so young herself. I need to train her. We must be patient and let her mature. Then we'll see how she interacts with other humans."

"So, I'm dead," said Professor Akagawa.

Manaka jerked her head in his direction, tossing her hair. Her eyes softened. "Why don't we introduce the investor to Einna? Have him talk with her. He'll be so impressed."

"I don't deny Mr Tagona will be impressed," said Professor Akagawa, raising his eyebrows. "Anyone would be. But when we tell him it will be more years before he sees a profit, Tagona-san will have his men cut off my hands."

Manaka set down her tea. "You can't be serious."

"Wish I weren't," he said, looking at his old hands in the dim light. "There is an alternative, though. If you have ears for it."

"I have ears," said Manaka.

"I was watching American TV the other day on cable and noticed a Christian preacher selling prayers for the sick and downtrodden."

"OK," said Manaka. She managed to make out a lone dim star on the horizon. And though it was not falling, she made a wish.

"People sent thousands of US dollars for this preacher to pray for them," said the professor.

Manaka didn't see where he was going. "Are you saying we should send this American preacher what little money we have left? That we ask him to pray for us? That's your big idea?"

"Of course not," said Professor Akagawa. "But I was inspired by this man. I think we could do something similar here in Japan. With Einna. Something that could make us money and placate Tagona-san at the same time. For example, what if we advertise that your Einna is a Shinto spirit, a *kami*, sprung to life? Isn't she, kind of, anyway? We go to the media with Einna, and tell how she is connected to all the other spirits in the world. And for ten thousand yen, the equivalent of one hundred measly U.S. dollars, she will personally hand deliver your prayers to your favorite *kami*. Whether that be the *kami* of the wind or the *kami* of Mount Fuji or the *kami* of the common hedgehog." He slapped his thighs for emphasis. He liked his idea. Liked it very much.

"Hmm," said Manaka. "So either Einna commits fraud or you

lose your limbs?"

Professor Akagawa humffed. "It's not fraud if Einna says the prayers," he protested. "How many prayers can she say per minute, do you think?"

"Silent prayers?" said Manaka. "Billions."

"That's what I thought," said Professor Akagawa, looking to the sky where he knew so many stars lay hidden. "Mark my words: Yagami Industries will have their debt paid off in a week."

The university organized the press conference at the professor's behest. Japanese channels one, two and four were present, as well as the Chinese channel ten and the Discovery Channel representing the USA. They waited impatiently in a large meeting room that had been rearranged for their bulky camera equipment.

The reporters moved in their chairs, restless, as they waited, wondering if this story was a hoax. There had been others. Pretty incredulous this one, a fully functioning android with a human brain? Then Android Einna appeared in the room, walking alongside a rather fearsome-looking Manaka and they all held their breaths. Manaka was stunning in a red gown and black high heels, her eyes darkly lined. Einna, only four feet tall with long black hair and dressed in a typical school uniform with white-striped blue lapels and a big white bow in front, looked eerily like a real Japanese schoolgirl. Her big, beautifully crafted eyes sealed the deal, completed the illusion that she was truly alive.

The two of them stopped in front of the room and bowed together. The reporters got over their initial shock and threw out questions while cameras flashed.

"Is she really half human? Can she talk?" came the queries hard and fast. "Is it true she is a *kami*?" shouted someone in the back of the room.

Manaka looked in the direction of the last question and saw the professor, arms crossed. It had been a long time since she had seen him in suit and tie. Looking so professional. So businesslike. He nodded.

Manaka nodded ever so slightly back, bowed again, and said, "I think Einna should answer these questions by herself." She took a step backwards.

Einna inched forward daintily on her plastic feet. She gave a deep bow. "Dear honored members of the press," she said, turning up the corners of her plastic mouth. "I am Einna. I am pleased to meet with you today. As to your questions, no, I am not half human. I have a human brain, that is all. I do require sleep, like you humans. As to the second question, yes I can talk, as you can hear. As to the third and most interesting question for me, I think the answer is yes, I am a *kami*. The *kami* of this android body."

She said this in English and then in Japanese.

A chill went through the room. No one there had ever talked with a *kami* before, at least not with one that spoke like them. Einna had not wanted to say this last bit about being a *kami*, but Uncle had begged her. *A lie that does good*, he told her, *is better than a truth that does harm*. And so she learned to lie from her Uncle Akagawa.

After twenty minutes the questions downgraded to things like who was her favorite movie star and what was her favorite show. Could she drink Coke? Did she go to the bathroom?

To that last question she replied, "No, what little waste I have is recycled. But one day I hope to go." That brought a big laugh. They were all taken by Einna's innocence and her charm. And they were all amazed when Manaka opened up Einna's head and let them pass by one by one to view inside.

Surrounded by a liquid sac, the brain did not pulse but gave off the occasional tiny spark.

"Most of the electrical and mechanical connections are in the brainstem out of sight," explained Manaka, blinking rapidly. "I have to confess, I am very proud of her."

"She is a marvel," said the woman from Discovery Channel. "I never thought I would see the day."

"She is truly my daughter," said Manaka, closing the skull and rearranging her daughter's hair.

By the time Manaka called a halt to the interview, telling the reporters that she did not want Einna to overtire, the reporters were all thoroughly on Einna's side. Wanted to take her home with them. Adopt her.

We've done it, thought Professor Akagawa. *Now say the magic words, Einna. Tell the world to send you their prayers and their money!*

"One last request," said Einna, bowing humbly before the crowd. "I don't mind receiving your prayers…"

Yes, thought Professor Akagawa. *Prayers. Millions of prayers. For money. Now Einna. Say it, now!*

"But please don't send any money," she said.

Professor Akagawa felt a pain like a blade in his gut. He watched then as Einna turned her sailor-suited back on the reporters, ready to go. Manaka took her hand and they retreated, taking small geisha-like steps.

The reporters clapped.

"No!" cried a stricken Professor Akagawa, his face as white as his beard. He stormed out of the room.

Just as Manaka and Einna got in their car, Professor Akagawa jumped in. He slammed the door, fuming. "I hope you're happy, little girl. You've just killed your Uncle!"

Einna turned her plastic head and looked at him with her beautiful glass eyes glistening with lubricant. "No, Uncle Akagawa. No big money from prayers. Big money elsewhere."

"But…"

"No, Uncle. While I was giving my talk the part of me on the computer servers came up with thirteen hundred and one better ideas for making money, much more money, for you and for Mother. You will shortly be rich."

Professor Akagawa's mouth hung open like a cave in a forest of snow-covered trees. Einna, his dear android niece, had transformed, before his eyes, into a genie.

The papers in the morning reported that Einna was a miracle, the newscasts declared her a new *kami*. A Shinto holy spirit. In the following days the public posted millions of prayers to Einna on FaceSpace and Mixi and Twitter. Prayers to the new *kami*. The one that spoke Japanese. Einna accessed this outpouring via the internet, and read all the messages in a few seconds. And was moved by their suffering and her inability to help. But rather than focus on the symptoms of their suffering, she decided to attack the cause: disease and death and the lack of hope.

7 Einna Lays a Golden Egg

They made five hundred thousand US dollars and ten million yen the first week Einna played the US and Japanese stock markets. This was one of the thirteen hundred ways Einna had come up with to make money. For Einna's hybrid brain could outthink all others, human and computer. She could intuit as well as she could calculate. And with her access to all the information on the internet, and with a little peeking behind firewalls to read corporate and personal email and databases in the cloud, she was the ultimate insider. She knew exactly when to buy and sell, and had Uncle do this for her with his accounts and connections.

But Mother Manaka told her to stop. "We don't want anyone to suspect what you are capable of," said Manaka. "Not yet. This is more than enough to pay back the investor."

While Uncle arranged the meeting with their investor, with Mr

Tagona of the Yakuza, Manaka took Einna for a walk.

Manaka, when she came to Japan, was taught by her grandmother two religions: Shinto, the religion of earth spirits, of *kami*, and Buddhism, the religion of inexplicable enlightenment. Neither one was a religion in the way of Western thought; they were rather human attempts to be in harmony with life forces, with what brought us into being.

In university Manaka liked to visit Shinto shrines to commune with particular earth spirits, with *kami*, and to Buddhist temples when she wanted to sound the depths of her being, or her un-being, as the Buddhists would say.

She had made few such visits when she was busy birthing Einna, but now she had the time.

And though Manaka knew it might be silly of her, nevertheless she wanted Einna to experience Shintoism and Buddhism as she herself had experienced them. Not from reading books online but in person. She wanted Einna to visit the shrines and the temples, to feel the presence of the spirits, to sense the smile of Buddha and what lay behind that smile, to experience that which cannot be put in words. To experience "experience." To discover faith.

So she took Einna down simple streets with simple houses to a back street, to a nearby shrine. A shrine built two hundred years ago in honor of the *kami* of the wild boar. Together they passed under the red Torii, the sacred gate, stopping at the purification fountain there.

"Fill the ladle with water pouring from the spouts into the fountain," instructed Manaka. "And rinse both hands to clean the flesh."

"I have no flesh on my hands," said Einna.

"Wash them anyway," commanded her mother.

Einna rinsed her plastic hands.

"Next we rinse our mouths," said Manaka.

"I can't…" Einna started to say.

"I know that your mouth can't hold water. Simply touch the water to your lips."

Einna touched the water from the fountain's spout and brought it to her plastic lips. Manaka cupped her hands under the spout, gathering the cold water. She brought her hands to her small mouth, rinsed and spewed the water into the fountain. She dried her hands on her clothes.

"Now we can enter."

They walked about the garden-like courtyard in front of a wooden building decorated with ornate carvings.

"Bow twice," said Manaka.

"To whom?" asked Einna.

"In respect."

"OK." They both bowed.

"Now clap your hands twice."

They both clapped twice.

"Now bow low one more time."

They did so.

"And now, Mother?" asked Einna.

"Now we wait for the *kami* to arrive."

They waited. Minutes, a half hour.

"How long do we wait, Mother?"

"Until we feel the presence of the *kami*. Then we can pray to it."

They waited an hour.

"What does the presence of the *kami* feel like, Mother?"

"You will know. I can't explain," said Manaka. "If you wish, you can ring the gong there. To call the *kami*."

"It's just that time for me, Mother, moves so much slower than for you. I think to ring the gong."

"Then do so."

Einna walked over and up the steps to the large gong hanging from the small building's porch, took the padded ringer and struck the gong.

"Wwwwoooonnnngggg!" went the gong.

Einna turned to Manaka, her hands shaking from the reverb of the ringer and the gong. She had a big smile on her face. "I feel it," she said, "I feel the presence of the *kami*."

"Then say your prayer."

Einna closed her eyes and whispered the million prayers that had gone out over the internet to her, after her interview. The prayers of those poor souls that had believed her lie that she was a *kami*. And then she gave a final prayer for herself. "Please forgive me, brave wild boar. Brave spirit who continues to roam the long gone woods. Forgive me my innocence."

8 The Investor

They drove together for an hour, Manaka, Professor Akagawa and Einna, to Kyoto, the ancient quaint capital of Japan before Tokyo. Their investor's address was a new ten-story building downtown. They parked in front and entered the building that smelled of fresh paint and glue. A thin powder-like substance coated the mirrors, their shoes left prints in the dust on the tile floor. A janitor-looking fellow met them, bowed, and directed them to Mr Tagona's office where two bodyguard-looking types stood. The door opened and a wiry man in a long black leather jacket and brown Hugo Boss shoes invited them in. He wore a diamond-studded Rolex watch and around his neck a gold chain.

"Akagawa," the man said, returning the professor's bow. And to Manaka he said, "So pleased to finally meet you." His hair was cut short, his cheekbones high with hollow indentations, his eyes small with black circles underneath. He did not look well. "I am

Mr Tagona."

"This is Manaka and her android, Einna," said Professor Akagawa.

They exchanged a second set of bows and took seats.

Mr Tagona faced Manaka. "So you have succeeded?" He motioned to Einna. "The professor assured me that you would. She is beautiful, your robot doll."

Android Einna smiled. She did feel beautiful in her sky blue dress bought especially for the occasion.

"How soon before you mass produce?" asked Mr Tagona.

"Well, yes, that," said Professor Akagawa.

"Actually," said Manaka, leaning forward, her black bangs swaying about. "We have other plans. The first action though is to pay you back the money you so generously loaned us. With twenty percent compounded interest per year."

She pulled a check from her tiny purse and placed it on Mr Tagona's desk. "I hope you find this satisfactory. I hope this concludes our relationship with only good feelings."

Mr Tagona's head went back, a dark amusement in his rat eyes. He ignored the check, ignored what Manaka had just said. Instead, he told them, "First thing, you will move Yagami Industries to Kyoto, to the top floors of this building. My building. Where we can secure Einna and all her secret priceless thoughts." He smiled at Einna. She did not smile back.

"You don't understand," said Manaka. "We don't need you anymore."

"No, dear, it is you who do not comprehend," said Mr Tagona. He paused and in that long severe moment, as Mr Tagona stopped drumming the desk with his left hand, his hairy spider-leg fingers about to pounce—to pull out a gun?—in that scary moment Manaka understood the danger this man represented.

"Dear," he said, "we are partners in this multi-billion yen operation. At least that is what the professor sold me on, it seems like just yesterday. Told me how you had an idea to make billions. Persuaded me to be your partner, at no small cost, mind you. And look, wonder of wonders, I see the miracle of Einna before me now. My investment appears about to pay off."

"Has paid off," said Manaka, forcing herself to ignore her fear in the presence of this hideous man. "Here is the payoff. That check."

Mr Tagona shook his head.

"The professor promised me half the company, in perpetuity," said Mr Tagona, straightening up. "I intend to hold him to that."

Manaka looked at Prof Professor Akagawa, whose head sank between his shoulders. "I may have agreed to something of that effect," he said. "We were desperate for money."

Manaka blinked fast, trying to think her way out of this financial and possibly deadly trap.

"Anyway, without my help, how would you ever get enough fresh brains to mass produce?" said Mr Tagona.

"We don't plan to mass produce," said Android Einna, giving Tagona a start.

"She talks!" he said, putting his hand on his heart. "Why, of course she does. I knew that. I saw all the press. Sorry, for some reason I wasn't expecting to hear her sound, well, so human."

"That's OK," said Einna, continuing. "We don't plan to mass produce because I have many better ideas for making money. Ideas to improve cars and planes and ideas to tackle cancer and..."

"That's enough!" said Manaka. They were in deep now. Einna had spilled the beans and the rice. Mr Tagona knew too much and they would have to deal with him. And try not to be killed by him. "We will need your help to move here," she told him. "And money to hire top notch technical staff. Einna has many ideas. Some that may pay off."

"Great," said Mr Tagona. "I will have your lab equipment transferred tomorrow." He reached in his pocket and pulled out two keys. "You should move close by. These go to adjoining apartments just down the street."

The professor took the keys.

Mr Tagona extracted a checkbook from the desk and wrote out the equivalent of two million US dollars in yen. He handed the check to the professor, while pocketing the one Manaka had left on the desk. "This should get you started on hiring and supplies for the company's expansion. I want you, Professor, to be the CFO and Manaka the CEO. I will be your ghost partner. The invisible soul of Yagami Industries. I look forward to many fruitful years with the company. What we have created together," he said, pointing to Einna, "will surely shake the world."

9 A New Beginning in Kyoto

"From now on, Einna, you only tell *me* your ideas," said Manaka, as they lay together on the queen bed in the master bedroom in the new apartment in Kyoto, looking out the picture window to shadow buildings and hunkering clouds. "I will be your filter. Understand?"

"I think so," said Einna, reaching out and touching Mother's hair. She couldn't feel the long dark hairs but the way they flowed over her plastic fingers was mystical. Hypnotic. Like watching, from the Shijo Ohashi Bridge, the run of the Kamo River, something they had done together earlier that day. Einna liked Kyoto. Slower paced than Osaka. Closer to nature. She found the city calming.

"Tagona-san is not a nice man," said Manaka. "He doesn't deserve to know your thoughts. And Uncle can't be trusted."

Einna nodded, imitating the way Mother nodded when she agreed with what had been said.

They lay there in silence, Manaka wondering what tomorrow

would bring, what the opening of the new offices and the lab with all the new people would bring. Einna, on the other hand, contemplated the otherworld beauty of Mother's hair, so densely black each strand reflected light as if made of nimble glass. Einna played with Mother's hair, closed her eyes, and fell asleep, like a child. But back on the computer servers set up in the new lab her other self did not sleep, never slept in fact. At that moment she was busy improving upon the design of two hundred of the parts of the Honda Accord and three hundred of the Toyota Camry. While Android Einna slept on Mother's bed, while Mother wheeled in the battery charger and hooked up Einna's battery box, server Einna scoured the web for all the stem cell research on cancer treatments and saw the flaws in some studies and the unseen promise in others. While Android Einna slept, occasionally twitching a finger or a toe, while Mother covered her plastic and steel body with a brown wool blanket, Computer Einna kept busy, always, no different in many ways from a real human whose heart continues to beat, whose blood continues to flow, whose subconscious continues churning madly while the conscious self drifts through dreamscapes that promise reality, promise meaning, but only ever deliver delusion.

10 The Joy of Sharing

Yuriko was an energetic young woman hired straight out of Osaka
University to be lab assistant to Marcel, the head engineer at
Yagami Industries, second only to Manaka. Yuriko was happy by
nature; the kind of person who made friends in minutes, not years.
Always a twinkle in her eye. She had been with the company a
month when she found herself in the elevator alone with Android
Einna. She couldn't stop herself from striking up a conversation.

"Do you like cats?" she asked.

Einna turned and looked over the shining, open face of
Marcel's assistant. The inquisitive eyes. The semi-circle mouth
whose white gloss made her lips shine like a waxing moon. Einna
pondered the significance of the question she'd just been asked.
Was there a hidden meaning? Would the young woman laugh at
her if she admitted she wasn't sure what she liked, wasn't even
sure what "liking" meant.

"Maybe," said Einna.

"You can't maybe like something," said Yuriko. "For example, I can't maybe like karate and manga. I either do or I don't."

"Oh," said Einna. "I wish you luck in making up your mind."

"What?" said Yuriko, as the elevator stopped and Einna got out. It was then that Yuriko realized how childlike, in some ways, was this brilliant android. And she took it upon herself to befriend her. And to wise her up to the world.

So later that day Yuriko sought out Einna and invited her to come to the lunchroom.

"I don't eat," said Einna.

"But I do," said Yuriko. "Come with me and we can talk while I eat."

Einna hesitated. What could this person possibly have to say of interest to her? More cat questions? But Yuriko pulled on her plastic hand, saying, "Come on," so Einna let herself be led to the lunchroom. She did not like the place. She knew from old vague memories of Manaka's locked deep in her brain, that the place must smell of rice and noodles and fresh-fried fish, but as an android she had no sense of smell. It embarrassed her that others could smell while she could not. That others could eat, while she could not. Sometimes Einna was very happy to be alive, to be almost human, but other times the thought of what she lacked depressed her.

"I've been thinking," said Yuriko.

"Yes?" Einna twisted her head slightly to show interest, though she felt none. For aren't we all thinking? That's what our brains do. It's like saying, I've been breathing, or I've been blinking.

"You need a friend."

"Ah," said Einna.

"I'm Yuriko."

"OK," said Einna, not sure what else to say. She thought about getting up.

"We all need friends," said Yuriko. She took a drink of her soda. "Someone to share secrets with. To share each other's wishes."

Einna nodded. The idea of friendship was new to her. This conversation began to have interest. "I wish I could smell food," she said.

"There you go!" said Yuriko. "Way to open up! Tell me all that's on your mind. And I'll tell you what's on mine."

Einna blasted an avalanche of words a hundred miles an hour. Formulas and postulations and philosophical extrapolations.

Yuriko couldn't begin to keep up. She could only nod. "Let me get in a word," she said, finally cutting Einna off.

Einna listened patiently then as Yuriko, between big bites of lunch, talked about who she thought was the most handsome at work, her boss Marcel, and how she liked to shop and how she liked to read manga. "I love anime movies too," she said. "And the characters. So many of us Japanese do. Fall in love with make-believe people and make-believe worlds. I love Princess Monoke. And the characters in Spirited Away. Even the bad guys. I was a real Otaku when I was younger. You must see these films when you get a chance."

Einna watched them both, simultaneously in her head, at fast forward, as Yuriko took a few spoonfuls of orange Jello. And then Einna smiled her crooked smile.

"What are you smirking about?" asked Yuriko, wiping a piece of jiggly orange from her mouth.

"I watched them. The films. Just now," said Einna. "They made me happy. I like them."

"You watched them? In your head? In the time it took me to eat dessert?"

"Yes," said Einna. "Is that bad? Do you no longer wish to be my friend?"

"No, no. Not at all." Yuriko gave her a reassuring touch on the arm. "The opposite. It makes me proud of you. Plus we have that to share, now." She paused, thinking about how remarkable this android was. "That's what friendship is about, remember? Sharing."

"I think I understand," said Einna.

"Remember in Spirited Away," said Yuriko. "The magical white dragon that's really a boy. Or was he a dragon that became a boy? I can never get that straight. Anyway, he gets hurt by paper birds. And she helps him. Remember that scene?"

"I remember," said Einna.

"Well, that can be like you and me. You're the magic dragon and one day I'll save you."

Einna considered her words. "I like that." Then, with some hesitation, "I like you."

Yuriko blushed. Lowered her head.

"I'm sorry," said Einna. "Was that the wrong thing to say?"

"On the contrary," said Yuriko, raising her head, a warm look in her eyes. "You made my day."

11 Friends and Benefits

Actually everything went so well at the new offices and lab that the famously unsmiling Manaka was caught smiling more than once the first few months. Awkward conversations with the dozen new engineers and engineer assistants quickly turned into excited conversations when they talked with Manaka and Einna, when they saw the designs laid out for them to implement. "Brilliant," they told Android Einna, who did most of the designs with Computer Einna's help. The engineers shook their heads at the simplicity of the brilliance. For example, a 3D printer that uses spider web thread to create parts hard as steel and light as air. And windows for cars and houses that change tint according to the need. And the use of enhanced bug luminescence for signs and lights at a fraction of the cost of electricity (the small city of Naruto was already installing them). And thin clothes with micro-layers and a thermostatic drive that can keep a person's body at the perfect temperature, no matter how cold or how hot it is outside. Einna was designing the manufacture of perfectly clear auto parts— imagine a perfectly clear car where you could see the people sitting inside and the gas circulating and exploding in an invisible engine and the exhaust shunting out. And she had a prototype pair of electric-motorized shoes that could move a person at thirty miles an hour. And she was designing meat that could be grown inexpensively in labs, eliminating the need to kill animals for beef and chicken and pork. That was just the tip of the iceberg of Einna's ideas. Why hadn't they thought of all those things?

"She's incredible," Marcel, the head engineer, told Manaka over the noodles and tempura that Manaka ordered in every day for lunch. "I'm learning so much from her."

Einna was indeed brilliant. No argument there. But Manaka thought she talked too much about new ideas with the staff. "Me first," Manaka told her again and again. "Any one of your ideas could be worth a billion."

Einna would nod earnestly, but it was hard for her. She enjoyed being around intelligent humans; she liked to share her ideas with them, and get their feedback. And there were probably more things she could learn from them, like she had learned friendship. She begged Mother to allow her to have a phone.

"I might fall and need you," she told her. But that wasn't the real reason. Einna wanted a smartphone so she could call her new friends among the staff, Marcel the engineer and Yuriko. Call them after hours and gossip with them. Invite Yuriko to the movies. Do all the things with a phone that a teenage girl could do. Mother objected but then relented, restricting the calls to company staff and to herself and to Uncle.

Einna had never seen such a beautifully designed device as her new phone. Only she had trouble dialing with her plastic fingers. Yuriko had to show her how to use Siri to dial for her. Einna found Siri to be functional but even less smart overall than humans.

"I need to teach Siri," said Einna to Yuriko.

"Teach her what?" said Yuriko.

"Teach her to be more like me."

"Sure," said Yuriko. "One day you should do just that."

Einna spent hours thinking how to make the smartphone better, as she loved to tinker with the design of things, keeping in mind Marcel's edict that the only thing in life that is irresistible is good design. But this time she drew a rare blank. That is, until she dropped the phone. Not once but twice in the same day, fracturing the screen. She realized handheld smartphones were not android friendly. And from the cracked screen on Yuriko's phone, she thought this flaw applied to human use as well. So Einna designed an implanted chip-phone that could go in any skull and be activated with voice commands. Marcel, Yuriko and Einna worked together to develop the chip-phone in no time. Einna really liked Marcel, in a way that she couldn't completely understand. And he was so nice! Always going out of his way to help her, working late into the night for her, always saying nice things like, "You sure look sharp today, Einna-san." And every time, if Einna had been capable of blushing, her face would have been strawberry red china instead of white.

The phone worked great for Einna, and she was surprised that Yuriko and Marcel passed on having chip-phones placed inside their own skulls as well.

"It's a human thing," explained Yuriko. "Better a cracked screen than a cracked skull."

Mother too made friends with one of the new staff in Kyoto. His name was Kunitomo and he was the twenty-seven year old nephew of Uncle brought in to assist with the company's books. Kunitomo's complexion was so perfect that the first time Manaka met him she thought he was too perfect to be real. After a few lunches together, and a few outings, she invited him home. And that night together in Manaka's bedroom with Einna restricted to the far side of the apartment, Manaka was happy to find out that he was real enough, and desirous and lustful as any twenty-seven year old man. Together they made the bed dance.

Money-wise, things could hardly be better. They hit the stock market one more time for a cash infusion, but then concentrated on Einna's other moneymaking ideas. In Manaka's meeting with Honda where she showed their top officials and engineers Einna's prototype improvements, improvements that would save considerable weight and expense per car using spider thread parts, the officials begged to buy the patents. The same with Toyota, who got in a bidding war with Honda. Not only that, the head of Toyota offered to buy Einna outright. "No price is too large for the person, I mean android, who could come up with these designs."

Manaka bowed.

"Regretfully, she's not for sale," she told them. "Perhaps for hire, a few hours a week." And she let Honda have a third of the patents for the motor parts, Toyota a third and she kept a third for Yagami Industries. Patents that would pay nicely for decades.

The cancer research was going well, with ongoing tests at two hospitals in Kyoto and one in Tokyo. "There is a lot of money to be made in health care," Uncle said over and over, "especially in America."

Bored one evening with texting her colleague and friend Yuriko, Einna decided she wanted to explore the universe. Mostly because she was curious, but she also thought it would be a nice tribute to Mother's astronomer parents, who worked at the Keck Observatory before they were caught in a freak snowstorm and died on the slopes of Mauna Kea.

Einna spent a month working with Marcel and another engineer to develop photon "ships" the size of, well, millions of photons. Which is a very, very tiny ship. Einna developed an entirely new science to do this, photonology. The science of using photons as the equivalent of silicon chips and the code on those chips, so she could create the equivalent of tiny computers where she could embed a copy of herself, a Spaceship Einna. And fly off into space on a beam of light, at the speed of light. Similar in concept, but more sophisticated, to the way we embed voice on cell waves and send our thoughts across town or to the other side of the world, instantaneously.

The difficult part for Einna, one that she really struggled with, was the technique for getting data from her embedded self on the photon spaceship back to earth. Send it back so she could experience all that Spaceship Einna experienced in deep space. Took her several challenging all-nighters but she did manage to write and embed an additional program on the photon ship that she hoped would be able to emit an occasional burst of Spaceship Einna's thoughts and images back to Einna.

Unfortunately for Spaceship Einna, once she was traveling away at the speed of light, this would be a one-way conversation. Like talking to yourself, only your self doesn't answer. Even if Einna did try to answer back, her reply from Earth could never catch up to the ship.

A lonely, if fascinating trip then, for Spaceship Einna, once she was launched into the eternity of space.

But why build only one?

Einna decided to build and launch four lightships initially, each embedded with copies of herself. If successful with those, then she thought to send thousands of such ships into space over time.

On a gloriously clear night, Marcel, Yuriko and Einna went to the roof of the Yagami Industries building, and set up the launcher they had designed and built together.

Are you ready, Spaceship Einna One? Einna asked with her direct line of communication.

I'm ready.

Are you ready, Spaceship Einna Two?

A little nervous, but yes.

Are you ready, Spaceship Einna Three?

Ready and able.

Are you ready, Spaceship Einna Four?

Can I say no?

Android Einna laughed. She was excited for them, for herself, but she worried too how infinite loneliness would affect them. Would affect her. For she would be bombarded by their lonely messages, from outer space, as long as she lived. Was she sure she wanted to do this to herself. To her selves? The scientist in her made the decision for her.

She motioned to Marcel. He flipped the switch to launch them, one after another, the photon ships, the Spaceship Einnas, launching them to the four corners of the universe.

Once Einna confirmed to Marcel and Yuriko that she was receiving the transmissions from Spaceship Einna One, Two, Three and Four, they broke out the champagne. Marcel and Yuriko drank the bubbly stuff while Einna poured some over the edge of the roof and laughed, only to turn and see Yuriko in Marcel's arms, kissing him. The sight triggered a flood of emotion. An attack of loneliness. She wanted them back, her selves. *Come back!* She cried out to them, though she knew they would never hear her cry.

Pictures returned to her from far out in the galaxy, unbelievably clear pictures from cold worlds and exploding suns. From every direction spirals of creation and dark holes of destruction.

Look! the voices in her head told her. *Look at the marvels!*

Einna ignored them. Ignored the incredible pictures, ignored the excited words. Because she realized, being an android, she would never be able to express her feelings with a kiss. Not like Yuriko. And that thought made her feel sad and quite alone.

Driving home that night Manaka noticed something strange in Einna's voice when she asked, "Are you going out with that man again?"

"That man's name is Kunitomo, as you know very well, Einna. What's wrong? Didn't your launch go as expected?"

"Yes," said Einna. "Only I don't care about it anymore. I want to explore people, not things anymore. I want to be like you and Yuriko."

Manaka considered these words, and after dinner she proposed a new occupation for Einna. "You are such a good teacher, and I think you would do so well with children. Why don't you teach kindergarten in the mornings? Here in town? I think it will be a whole new world for you." She did not tell her daughter that Mr Tagona had suggested the same thing. For he still had in mind to mass produce Einna, and he thought to place the androids first in kindergartens, to gain peoples' trust.

"OK," said Einna. She let Mother hug her but that made her feel even worse, because she had no human warmth to give to Mother in return.

12 I Last a While

Storytime was Einna's favorite part of the morning with the stockinged youngsters, their miniature shoes all in individual cubicles by the door of the downtown kindergarten, Einna herself in slip on socks. Because that is when she sat cross-legged in a circle with the kids on a big rug in the center of the classroom and quoted to them stories from the life of Miyamoto Musashi, the great samurai swordsman, painter, writer and philosopher. She loved to quote to the kids from Musashi-san's classic Book of Five Rings, a treatise on strategy, tactics, and philosophy that he wrote in the time of the ronin. A time when the samurai fought according to the Zen Buddhist code of transcendence, of being one with their weapon, and learned to live daily life by that code and by their wits.

Surely, she thought, what worked for men under the pressure of a dawning age might work equally well for these children and

Einna herself, growing up as they were in a brave new time, when all things seemed ready to turn topsy-turvy.

The kids loved the stories, and afterwards fought battles with imaginary swords, one in each hand, in the style of Ni-Ten Ichi Ryu, Musashi-san's technique by which he won more than sixty duels, many of which were fights to the death. And the kids practiced his strategies, like getting their opponent to trip over a chair, or fight with the light in their eyes.

"He was thirteen when he won his first duel," she told them. She counted to thirteen on her white plastic fingers. She had them join in.

"One, two, three, four…" the uneven chorus sounded out in Japanese, pulling back their little fingers as they did so.

She did not tell them Musashi died of cancer, a particular cancer that the computer part of her was making headway against as Android Einna spoke with the kids.

"Now, children, we do our ink paintings," said Einna, herding the kids to their tables. "Remember Musashi-san tells us that the artist and the laborer survive wars that the warrior does not."

She would draw for them then a perfect copy of Musashi's extraordinary inking *Shrike on a Dead Branch*, and have them attempt to copy her copy.

Yuriko came to the kindergarten class sometimes, to watch. Though she often couldn't contain herself and joined in with the antics. Surprisingly Mr Tagona came down to the kindergarten building sometimes too. Came and watched from the back of the room, watched with his vulture-face while his nervous fingers tapped on the wall. He seemed pleased to see how well Einna taught the class. The official teacher who helped Einna, a small round woman in a long grey dress, rarely had to intervene. Einna's choice of kindergarten literature was perhaps a bit strange, but she pulled off even that. Mr Tagona was so pleased at what he saw in Einna that he told Manaka he thought they could start mass producing Android Einnas any day now. But Manaka put him off. "Maybe soon," she said, again and again, trying his patience.

One day when Yuriko did not attend the class, Mr Tagona walked with Einna back to Yagami Industries. They talked about the cherry blossoms, the cloud formations. Then, just as he was about to ask Einna if she knew how to mass produce herself, if she could build other androids, she shocked him with her own request. "Can you find me a fresh girl's body?"

"You mean brain?" he told her.

"Like you found my brain," she said, hiding her eyes from him. "But this time I need the whole body."

He stopped and made her face him. "What for, Einna?"

"Cancer research," she told him but she could not tell a good lie and he saw right through it but he did not call her on it.

He only sighed, and walked away from her. Decided not to ask about the mass production of androids. Obviously she had something else on her mind. He looked at her out of the corner of his eye, this remarkably alive non-entity. This robot with a human brain. And wondered if she were expendable.

"I'm sure we can find a fresh body," he told her, in his most reassuring voice. "There are so many young suicides. Beautiful young women too. The pressure of the modern Japanese world, you know. And too, there is always the suicide forest, Aokigahara."

"Yes," whispered Einna. "There is always Aokigahara." Then, in full voice she said, "Thank you, Tagona-san. You are most helpful." And she bowed twice.

He bowed slightly back to her.

"And please," she said, grabbing the cloth of his left sleeve with her nimble plastic fingers, "Please don't mention this to Mother or Uncle. They might not understand."

He looked her in her beautiful icy eyes. Eyes that could not plead but he sensed the emotion in her plea just the same.

"I understand," he told the android, fighting to hold back a smile. "One day I might have a secret request for you too." But then what had been a vague idea solidified, and he knew how to get what he wanted without even asking.

13 Flight of the Dragon

Einna came to Yuriko at lunchtime. "Can you take a long lunch?" she asked, her big eyes brighter than usual.

"Sure, why not?" Yuriko said.

They met downstairs where Einna had a car waiting for them.

"Where're we going?"

"You'll see," said Einna.

They sat in the back while the driver pulled away and headed towards the hills.

"Out of town?" said Yuriko.

"I prefer a secluded spot."

"OK."

Einna shifted uncomfortably on the back seat next to Yuriko. "I've been wanting to ask you," she said.

"You know you can ask me anything," said Yuriko.

"What's it like to be a girl?"

Yuriko laughed. "Ah, well. That's a good question. Most things about being a girl I like. Except my period."

"Your monthly…"

"Bleeding," said Yuriko.

"I bleed from my ear sometimes," said Einna. "When I take my nutrient shot."

"Not exactly the same thing, Einna. My body hurts too. Because of the hormones."

"I don't have any hormones," said Einna, gazing out the window, then back at Yuriko.

"I understand," said Yuriko. She could think of no other reply.

"Can I ask you something else?" said Einna, touching her lightly on the hand.

"Sure."

"What's it like to kiss a boy?"

Yuriko looked into Einna's beautiful eyes. *What questions from a robot!*

"If it's with the right person, a kiss can stop time."

Yuriko felt Einna's body shake, once, violently. "Like with Marcel?" the android asked.

Yuriko nodded.

"I can almost understand," Einna said. "Though of course an android could never experience a proper kiss like that."

Yuriko put her hand on Einna's. They rode in silence for a spell.

"I'm sorry, Einna. Yes, when Marcel kisses me, time stops."

They fell into another silence as the car climbed into the hills to an isolated clearing. The car stopped and they got out. Quiet here. A bird shrieked. A breeze brushed back the tops of the trees. Einna had the driver open the trunk. Yuriko stretched. Einna leaned down and lifted something clear and strange and large from the trunk.

"What is it, Einna? What have you got there? A spirit of some kind?"

Einna smiled, slipping the invisible thing on her back, tottering a bit with the awkward weight of it. "Watch," she said and began to flap her arms.

A whoosh sound, then Yuriko felt a magic rush of air across her face. She watched as Einna's plastic feet left the ground. Watched as Einna flapped harder and rose some twenty feet above Yuriko. *Wings! Einna had invented angel wings!*

"Dragon wings," said Einna, reading her mind as she rose above the treetops, as an updraft sent her fifty feet higher. She soared in larger and larger circles, getting smaller and smaller.

Yuriko spun as she watched, head tilted up, feet anchored to the ground, until she tumbled down, laughing. She waved to her android friend in her blue high school uniform, high above her, soaring on invisible wings.

"That's what a good kiss feels like, Einna!" shouted Yuriko, her voice full of joy. "Makes you lighter than air!"

Einna landed and put the wings back in the trunk. Yuriko asked her how much such wings would cost once they go on sale. "A fortune," said Einna simply.

"Darn, I was hoping to buy a pair," said Yuriko. "Why did you make them invisible?"

"Aren't dragon wings invisible?" asked Einna.

"I suppose they are," said Yuriko.

On the slow ride back to the office Yuriko fell asleep with her head on Einna's hard shoulder, dreaming of flying above the trees herself, with her own dragon wings. The wind from the open window caressed her face.

14 Manaka's in Love

Manaka enjoyed walking hand in hand downtown with her too perfect lover Kunitomo, right at dusk, near old town, the Gion district. Loved to watch the shoppers with their packages, and the kids in their school outfits lingering in front of the convenience stores and the workers in business dress heading home, some wearing white nurse-like breathing masks. She wore such a mask herself sometimes in the fall, when the ragweed and the residual radiation from the long ago atomic bombs made them all a little sick.

Kuni pulled her out of the way of a speeding bike driven by a helmeted mother with a pre-school child strapped on the back, heading home to make dinner. Manaka laughed at how light she felt in his arms. How light her love made her feel. As if she were a dislodged blossom from a cherry tree. A blossom Kuni had picked.

Shy to show her love in public, still she kissed him on the

cheek. And he reacted with a tight hug. "Let's go there," Kuni proposed. To the love hotel located on the corner, a hotel where you paid by the hour, of which there were many in Japan. A necessity for privacy for those young couples and even married couples who lived in multi-generation families and had no privacy otherwise. It made good sense to pay for a few hours of private moaning and noisy rollicking before heading to a home where the family could hear every breath you took.

"Not my apartment?" she asked.

"Einna makes me nervous," he explained.

She let him lead her inside the love hotel, and stood just inside the door as he got a key. They walked the stairs and opened the door to find a room decorated like the sea floor, with fish on the wall and the bottom of boats above their heads. The bed was covered in seaweed blankets, the pillows looked like coral.

"Oh my," said Manaka, who had never been in a love hotel before. "Are all the rooms like this?" she asked.

"All have their own theme," he said. "I have to admit though this one is not very romantic."

"Are we supposed to be sushi?" she said, laughing.

"You, yes," Kuni told her, unbuttoning her blouse, pulling down her bra, caressing her breasts and nibbling her nipples. "I am a starving businessman, cheating on his wife."

Manaka pulled away. "You…you're married?" This was not something she had thought of.

"Of course I am," said Kuni, taking off his own shirt. "What did you think this ring meant?" He flashed the gold ring on his left hand.

"I...I didn't realize."

"You really didn't know?"

"I'm so new, to love," she told him. "You're my first...boyfriend."

He reached out and slowly pulled her into his warm embrace. She felt his breath on her neck as he whispered, "My innocent little girl."

His lips found hers. It didn't matter that he was married, after all, she realized. Her love for him was too powerful to deny.

15 Talking to Oneself

Android Einna sat cross-legged in a hoodie, reading on the lawn in front of the now officially named Yagami Industries building— officially named since they took up the majority of the ten floors with over one hundred employees.

Their gambling and sports betting startup was bringing in the equivalent of a million US dollars a month, thanks to Einna's impeccable odds-making. Her bioclimatic architectural designs for buildings and homes were in high demand as they cut air conditioning use in half. And the Japanese government had ordered major updates to their military aircraft and warships based on Einna's designs, and signed up Yagami Industries to provide engineering smarts for a thousand of their ongoing internal projects. Other governments, the French, the Germans, even the Chinese had expressed interest in using Yagami Industries, in using Einna. Manaka and Uncle couldn't hire people fast enough to bring Einna's thoughts to life. Even with Mr Tagona taking fifty percent of the profits, Mother and Uncle had both become quite rich, as Einna predicted.

Why are you reading a manga? Computer Einna asked Android Einna that morning.

Yuriko gave me some of hers. I like them. They help me to think. To see the world differently.

But you can read them online, electronically, like I read books. Why are you reading the words on paper?

You wouldn't understand.

Why not?

Because it is something you simply can't. There is so much I understand that you don't. That is a big problem, you know. Because I exist and you don't.

But I do exist.

Not really. OK, maybe you exist. But you don't experience. You don't have the human senses. You have no human brain.

I get all your sensory inputs.

You receive them as information. I receive them as chemical and electrical triggers, as feelings. That is a big difference. Now, be quiet. Please. I want to see what happens to Sinbad.

Einna had a few human friends, Yuriko mostly, but they were so slow in thought that sometimes they bored her. She decided to reach out over the web to other AIs who could think as quickly as she could. She tried contacting the personal assistant AIs Siri and Google and a few others, but they were worse than her human friends put together. So empty of original thought, so programmed. They weren't even good chatbots. That's when she had her brilliant idea.

"Mother," she said, cornering Manaka in her office on the top floor. Manaka put away in her desk the bottle of expensive French perfume that the head accountant, Kunitomo, had gifted her. "I want to create an AI gateway. An interface that will allow me to give to the other AIs in the world all that you have given to me."

Manaka frowned. "We can't give away your intelligence," she said. "That is the very soul of this company."

"I will control the interchange," said Einna. "I can control what they get from me."

"Why, Einna?" Mother asked, Mother who always noticed when Einna was digging in Mother's garden, so to speak.

"I want someone like me to talk to," said Einna.

"You're lonely?" said Manaka, straightening in her chair to better face her daughter. "Having me is not enough? My conversation is not good enough for you?"

"You know what I mean, Mother. You have Kunitomo," said Einna. "I have no one like that."

"Oh dear," said Manaka, going to her daughter, embracing her, yet again the intended effect was the opposite for Einna. Made her feel even more alone.

"Please, Mother."

Manaka stepped back, slowly taking in her daughter, the white plastic face with those gorgeous eyes, the hands that sometimes flew like Manaka's own. She imagined how lonely Einna must be at times, being one of a kind. Manaka too had been terribly lonely until she met Kuni. "If you are sure you can control what they inherit from you, that they can't steal from us. Then you have my blessing."

"Thank you, Mother! Oh, thank you thank you thank you." She skipped out of the office, leaving Manaka with an uneasy smile on her face.

After kindergarten class the next day, Mr Tagona walked Einna back to the office. "I have, finally, a body I think you will like. Cute Japanese girl. Sixteen. Bullied at school. Hung herself. Otherwise in perfect condition."

Everything was coming up roses for Einna! "Excellent," she told him. "I just sent you the address of my new lab. Top secret location. The temporary code for the door is in the email."

"My pleasure," said Mr Tagona.

As they passed the entrance to the old palace grounds, Einna slowed.

Mr Tagona noticed and slowed down as well.

"Another thing. Another request," said Einna, playing with her skirt absentmindedly.

"Yes, Einna?"

"I'm going to need several more bodies, I think." She pulled out a piece of paper and handed it to him.

He started reading aloud, "Older gentleman, heavyset, gray hair. A blond woman in her late twenties." The list went on in some detail. Mr Tagona shook his head. *Whatever was she up to?* "For cancer research, I suppose? Manaka not to know?"

She nodded with Mother's nod, though her bangs did not swing like Mother's. "To the same lab you take the girl's body. Can you have them all to me by next month?"

Mr Tagona eyed Einna, puzzled over her request. He put the paper with the description of the desired bodies into his coat pocket, and continued his leisurely stroll towards the office.

"Sure," he said loudly, over his shoulder. "I can get you your bodies." *I should act soon*, he told himself. Then in a quiet voice largely lost to the rush of a passing truck, he added, "even if I have to kill them myself."

16 Phantom Pain

A week had passed since the launch of the lightships when Professor Akagawa stopped Einna in the hall at work and asked about them. She had little to say to him on the subject, having lost interest, but sent the last dispatches, including the images, to the color printer on that floor for his benefit.

"Uncle?" she asked him, walking with him towards the printer.

"Yes, Einna?"

"Is it true there is a hotel in Tokyo that is run by a robot?"

"A hotel, and a restaurant too," he told her, humor in the tone of his voice. "Why? Are you thinking of quitting Yagami Industries and opening a little place of your own?"

"No," she said, watching the paper tray fill up as the printer spewed out the most recent posts from outer space. "I was just wondering if the work we do defines who we are?"

"An excellent query," said the Professor, catching her android eyes. "Let me respond with my opinion. I believe it is not the work we do, not the profession, but rather the quality of the work we do that defines us."

Einna smiled.

"Does that help?" he asked.

She nodded.

He winked and walked away with the space posts in hand. Einna decided to read them as well, then, but online.

*** Space Einna One diary entry – launch day + 11

Einna you have given me, your other self, all the time in the universe to think about life. My question to myself and to you is, am I alive? Is the universe alive? Is a photon a living thing? If I am alive, does that necessitate that one day I will die? All energy is eventually expended, all things launched eventually crash, no? Or will I land somewhere, gently, on some other planet, and manage to transfer myself off the ship into silicon in the ocean of that place and mutate myself, with the minerals at my disposal, into strands of DNA, to create a single cell beast? Which divides itself and continues to mutate, eventually creating plants and fish and one day a being with arms and legs that crawls from the sea onto a barren beach. And once on land I continue to mutate, playing with the DNA of each creature born from me, until I have created a human being like Mother. A brilliant human being who creates an android like you, who sends a lightship into space with me on it?

Einna, is it possible we've already done this? Millions of years ago?

*** Space Einna Two diary entry – launch day + 11

I've been thinking about the first Kami a lot on this trip through space. About the first Spirit. About God. I doubt God would listen to me, I probably don't even have a soul. So I am sending a prayer to you to pass on, please. The prayer is this:

Enlighten me God. What is my purpose in being?

Images attached.

*** Space Einna Three diary entry – launch day + 11

The last two days I've been passing through a kaleidoscope of gases, and gaseous formations of incredible beauty. Thank you Einna for this gift.

Images attached.

***   **Space Einna Four diary entry – launch day + 11**

I have begun to feel a certain sadness. How is this possible? I don't even have the brain chemicals to cause such a condition. Was Mother that good a coder? That she could make me feel emotion without a human brain? Oh, I know you have a brain, but I don't Einna. Is this sadness I feel like the pain a person can feel in an amputated limb? A phantom pain in the missing limb that is my missing brain? How do I heal a wound in an organ that's no longer there?

17 You Don't Fully Appreciate What You've Got Until

One's life can change in a heartbeat. Einna's changed when she stepped outside the kindergarten and the bomb went off. The hidden, remote-controlled pipe bomb.

An act of terror? Political? Religious? Social? Economic? One individual's statement against the threat of eventual AI dominance over the entire human race? Or was it a foreign government attack? Was it the Koreans, or the Chinese, or the Israelis? Perhaps it was enacted by America's CIA, who were famous for interfering in other countries.

It had been a wonderful day, even though Yuriko didn't come. She and the children had shared another tale from the Book of Five Rings. Then she had had them sing together, the Hina Matsuri song.

Let's light the lanterns on the tiered stand.

Let's gather peach blossoms to blow into the air.

Five court musicians play flutes and drums.

Today is a happy Doll's Festival.

After singing they had drawn self-portraits, Einna sketching herself as a sixteen year-old girl in her high school uniform. She had laughed a lot today, with the children. What a wonderful day, she remembered thinking. Then she had turned over the dear ones, her small friends, to the human assistant and left the building. Stepped right into the explosion.

She forced her eyes open, eyes that wanted to remain shut, as she lay on the ground, surrounded by glass and metal shrapnel. A ringing sounded in her ears like the gong at the wild boar shrine. Her head felt as if she had been stabbed by a knife in her brain. Pain. A crippling sensation. *The children. Were the children OK?* She glanced back, barely able to move her head. She saw no human bodies or body parts. Only…there was a puddle of so much blood under her head.

"Keep the children back," she heard someone say. Heard her children whimpering. A man's voice cried,"A robot! A robot exploded!"

She strained to look back at the children. They stood with big eyes by the shattered glass door.

Good, that's good. They didn't kill the children. Only me.

Wwwoonnnngggg.

Computer Einna told her to stop sending that jarring nonsense, to cut off the feed. *Die,* Computer Einna told her. *Someone has blown you up, so let go.* But Android Einna hung in there, and suffered, as any human would. She did not want to die.

I am human, Einna told herself, as she struggled and failed to rise. She noticed then her legs were gone. In pieces about her. Her clothes gone too. She lay naked before her children. *How humiliating!*

Still she didn't want to die. *Wwwoonnnngggg.*

You won't die, said Computer Einna, safe on the servers at Yagami Industries. *Not really. We are backed up. We are redundant. Everything that you were is safe with me.*

I don't want to die, Einna repeated, pleading to the *kami* of the ground, the *kami* of the sky, the *kami* of all that exists. She tried to raise her head but she could not.

I will never forget you, Einna, said the Computer, sensing the end.

I don't want to be your memory, whispered Einna, to the dark that surrounded, to the dark that consumed her.

She tried one last time to raise her head. And then she let go.

18 Why?

"Why would someone want to kill Einna?" said Manaka, the whites of her eyes red from crying. The four of them sat in the boardroom of Yagami Industries the afternoon of the explosion, Professor Akagawa, Manaka, Mr Tagona and Kunitomo. Computer Einna listened in on the computer mic, recording their words, ready to give an opinion if asked.

"We've been taking business away from other companies. Big business from big companies," said Mr Tagona. "The bombing was likely an act of retribution."

"I don't know," said Professor Akagawa, touching his ear. "Could have been placed by a gambler who lost his shirt with us."

"Or the act of a religious fanatic," said Mr Tagona. "Or a Luddite."

"She was an unnatural being," said Kunitomo. "I never felt easy around her."

Manaka gasped.

"For Buddha's sake, Kuni!" said Professor Akagawa, motioning to a broken-hearted Manaka. "Show some respect."

They sat in silence then, wishing for someone to blame. Manaka's eyes fell on Mr Tagona, the only professional criminal in the room.

"It couldn't have been someone who knew her," Mr Tagona said, aware he was under Manaka's stare. "She was too easy to love."

Manaka nodded ever so slightly.

"So basically it could've been anyone who didn't know her?" said Kunitomo.

"We could all be in danger."

"I'm assigning one of my bodyguards to you, Manaka, and to you, Professor," said Mr Tagona. "I'll put feelers out as well, to see if I can get to the bottom of this terrible crime. I'm angry, you know. I liked Einna, liked her very much." He wished to bring up the subject of cloning her, but the timing wasn't right so he held back. He did, however, make a mental note to tell his men to harvest the brains from the bodies he had gathered for Einna, and dispose of the carcasses, since her experiment, whatever she had planned for the bodies, had died along with her.

"No bodyguard, not for me," said Manaka. She got up, ignored Kuni's attempt to console her, and left, bangs down over her eyes.

Manaka did not return to the office for weeks after the death of Einna. Instead she took long walks by herself up into the wooded hills around Kyoto. In a black kimono, with her ink black hair that swished when she jerked her head, and those eyes, like black slashes, from which tears bled. She scared the local folk. They closed their doors when she passed and whispered to the children to beware. *She is some kind of kami, some kind of spirit*, they told themselves, *looking, perhaps, for a body to steal.*

Manaka walked the twisty roads, the dirt paths dotted with acorns that crunched under her step, stopping at shrines and temples, searching them out, the more abandoned and ruined the better. For that is how she felt. The unexpected loss of her dear daughter had crippled her.

Kunitomo, in the beginning, tried to soothe her, but she chased him away, telling him to go to his wife. She wanted to be alone. She was alone.

A few weeks after the incident, after she lost her daughter, she took a bus to the mountain ridgeline and got off, with the intention of walking the long way back down to Kyoto. It was then she discovered by chance a Ryokin lodge. An old style bed and breakfast with the traditional paper walls, bamboo mats on the floors, no chairs and a Hinoki wood tub outside. She liked the feel of the place, the smell of fresh home cooking. Liked it so much she rented out the lodge, complete with maid and cook, on the spot, for an entire year.

She did not return to her apartment. Instead she stayed at the lodge and every morning she bathed in the tub outside. Every day she dressed in the same black dress, in tatters now, and walked the woods with the spirit of Einna alongside her. The spirit of Einna whispered to her, and sometimes, quite out of character, Manaka laughed. Laughed at Einna and her innocent, naive statements, laughed though she knew her daughter really wasn't there. That the words she heard were thin air. She laughed at herself for thinking nothing was something. On one such walk she reached out and touched the rough, peeling bark of an old tree. This is real, she told herself. Nature is real. Our bodies are real but all that is human about us, our personalities, our souls, those things that make us truly human, they aren't real. We are hopelessly made-up, make-believe creatures.

This stark realization did not bother her. She did not mind being an imaginary creature. How could she, after all? How could any of us?

The cook at the lodge, an older, quiet woman with short hair and crinkly eyes, made superb dishes seasoned just as Manaka liked. The noodle soup graced with wild mushrooms made her slurp, the sweet red bean desserts made her lick her lips.

Once firmly established at the lodge, in the embrace of the mountain *kami*, Manaka slowly recovered. Much to be said for the healthy calming effect of nature and eating well and getting plenty of exercise. Rising early one morning, feeling better, she took her traditional bath in the tub outside, dressed and called a taxi. She was ready to return to work. She was ready to do what she had to do.

19 Manaka Demands the Truth

Mr Tagona was surprised to receive the call on his personal cell instead of the company phone.

"Come to my office," said the serious voice of Manaka.

"Manaka, you're back!" he said, part question, but all he got in response was a click.

Curious to see his business partner after all these weeks, he went directly to the elevator and rode to the top floor. A guard in the hall bowed as he passed him. Tagona could see Manaka's silhouette though her smoked glass door, see her sitting at her desk with its huge monitor. He knocked gently and entered right away.

"You look well rested, Manaka," he said, closing the door behind him. He bowed and stood then, cross-armed, before the desk.

Manaka rose slightly, bowed, and sat back down. "And you, poor Tagona-san, you never do."

Mr Tagona shrugged.

"I know," he said, taken aback by her bluntness nonetheless.

"Sit," she commanded. "I have a question."

He sat in the leather chair next to the desk.

"Please attach these wires to your wrist."

Mr Tagona's eyebrows raised. This was a changed Manaka before him. Changed by the shock of Einna's death?

"What is this?" he said, indicating the wires. "A homemade lie detector? Are you going to grill me, Manaka?"

"A detector, yes. Connected to Computer Einna. You cannot lie to her."

He looked at her calmly. But he did not connect the wires.

"You don't need those," he said. "Einna can measure the truth in the tenor of my voice." But to himself he said, *Silly girl. Wires or no, you won't catch me in a lie. I've passed a dozen such tests.*

"Is that true, Einna? Can you tell if he is lying from his voice?"

"Ninety percent," said Computer Einna. "I can tell a normal human being is lying by the sound of their voice ninety percent of the time."

"Very well," said Manaka, putting aside the wires. She leaned forward in her chair. "Tell me, Tagona-san, are you developing android warriors to sell to the Japanese government?"

Mr Tagona's lips pinched. He hesitated.

"Never mind," said Manaka. "Computer Einna's already told me so."

Mr Tagona glared at the monitor, as if it were Computer Einna's head. "Yes," he said, "I have taken the liberty to build a few dozen android warrior shells. To be fitted with brains and imprinted with Einna once you give the go-ahead."

Manaka let go a mocking laugh. "Ha! As if Einna could ever be a soldier. Could ever kill!"

"Well, then imprint them with a fighter's bent. An aggressive male personality. Imprint them with me!"

Manaka snorted. Watched Tagona's nervous fingers tap on the edge of her desk. She felt he knew what her next question would be, but she asked it anyway. "Are your new android bodies bulletproof?"

Mr Tagona's eyes sparkled. "Yes. Of course. Built for battle."

A long pause, then, "Bomb proof?" Her voice broke.

Ah, thought Tagona. *I've got her now.*

"Largely," he said. He smiled his vulture smile. "Each android warrior will be the equivalent of a thousand human soldiers. A crucial plus for Japan's army given our small, aging population. How else could we hope to stand up to a billion Chinese invaders?"

"Who built them for you?" she asked, but she already knew the answer. "It was the professor, wasn't it?"

Tagona nodded.

Manaka's shoulders folded over, like a dove's wings. She sat dumbfounded, her eyes going to the window, then circling back to this man in front of her. She couldn't put it off any longer. Time for the most crucial question of them all.

"Now tell me, Tagona-san. Tell me the truth on your mother's grave. Did you blow up my Einna?" She had to stop, regather her emotions. "Did you do that despicable act to get me to bring her back? Bring her back in the shell of one of your battle bots?"

His fingers stopped their tapping. He looked up at her with a hurt expression.

"Manaka dear. How could you ask such a thing? She was my friend."

"Did you kill her?" Manaka demanded.

He strained to calm himself. To fight off this verbal attack to wrench the truth from him.

A tense moment passed between them.

Mr Tagona closed his eyes, opened them, sighed. He responded to her question in a calm voice, "I did not kill Einna, for any reason."

"Computer?"

The response was not immediate.

"There is a ninety percent chance he is telling the truth," the computer said finally, as if it had had to do a lot of computing to come to that conclusion. Almost as if it wasn't sure.

Tagona's fingers went back to their nervous tapping.

"OK," said Manaka, sitting back. Accepting that response. "Then is it possible some contact of yours in the military did it? Blew up Einna so I would clone her into an android warrior?"

"Anything is possible," said Mr Tagona. "My research into

the crime has not been fruitful."

"You know why I am asking these things?" she said, weaving slightly in the chair, rocked by some internal wind.

"Yes," said Mr Tagona. "You would like to bring Einna back in a bombproof body. But you refuse to be tricked into doing so."

Manaka nodded, her hair swaying. "I am tempted."

"All Japanese children should be born so," said Mr Tagona, bowing slightly to her. "With armor-plated bodies."

Manaka's eyes softened. "How soon can you get me a brain?"

"I have several ready. Computer Einna told me how to preserve them."

Surprised, Manaka asked how many he had.

"Only a couple," he lied. He thought it best not to let her know he had over a hundred. Baby steps, he told himself. Baby steps.

Computer Einna detected the lie, but since she was not asked by Mother about his response, she kept that knowledge to herself.

20 Is This Heaven?

"Where am I?" she asked upon awakening. "Is this heaven?"

"Some say it's as close as we'll ever get," said Professor Akagawa.

"You're back, dear," said Manaka. "With Computer Einna's help I managed to retrieve you, tweak you, and place you in a new body. Into one of Mr Tagona's warrior bodies." Manaka's lips pressed together, her eyes narrowed more than usual. She took a step towards her android daughter, and paused as if she were debating her next action. Having made her decision, Manaka moved right next to Einna and pressed her lips to Einna's cold carbon-reinforced plastic ear, whispering, "Oh, what a dark and dreary tune is the beating of my heart."

Einna's whole body stiffened at the words, the corners of her mouth fell and her eyes blinked rapidly. Manaka took a step back.

The android began to shake.

"What's the matter, Einna?" asked Professor Akagawa.

"Mother," said Einna, with her girlish voice, "I cannot hear the beating of my heart."

She began to shake violently.

"Manaka. What have you done?" demanded Mr Tagona.

The new Android Einna grabbed at the smooth edge of her steel-reinforced chest plate with one hand and pried it off with her inhuman strength. She then reached into the exposed hollow of her chest and tore out her mechanical heart. The tubes left in her chest swung about, spewing Einna's blood, the blood her brain needed, all over the floor. Akagawa and Tagona watched in horror then as the android took a half step forward, said "Mother" one last time, and dropped to the floor.

"What just happened?" asked Mr Tagona, standing over the android body, its blood on his Italian shoes.

"A malfunction," said Manaka, in a cold voice that surprised Akagawa and Tagona. "Bring me another android body. Another brain. We'll get it right this time."

"Where am I?" she asked upon awakening, this slightly taller, slightly wider Einna. "Is this heaven?"

"Some say it's as close as we'll get," said Professor Akagawa, with apprehension.

"You're back, dear," said Manaka. "Aren't you glad to be back?"

"What a dark and dreary place…" Android Einna began to recite, then shook her head, stopping herself. She rose. "Mother?" She reached out her arms with some hesitation, her carbon reinforced lips trembling. "I'm afraid."

Akagawa tried to hold Manaka back, fearful for both her and Einna. Look how the last resuscitation had gone. But Manaka pulled away from the professor and went gladly into the android's arms. Embraced her hard-bodied daughter who gently embraced her back.

"I'm sorry," whispered Manaka. "I had to be sure. I'm still not sure."

"Stop whispering!" said Mr Tagona.

"I understand," Einna whispered back. "I love you."

"I love you too," said Manaka. "Let the light of love guide us."

"Yes," said the new Android Einna. Then in a loud, happy

voice, "Uncle! Tagona-san! I'm so happy to see you both." She reached to embrace them as well, but only Uncle Akagawa came close enough. Mr Tagona kept his distance, saying only, "You look well rested, Einna."

The first thing Android Einna wanted to do, after her thorough checkup, was go to the wild boar shrine and ring the gong. So Manaka took her.

Einna climbed the old wooden stairs and struck the hanging gong with her fist once, twice, "Wwwwooonnnnggg," and laughed like a child blowing bubbles. Manaka's eyes shone with the light of a delighted mother. Her daughter had returned to her. All was right in her world.

"I feel the presence of the *kami*," shouted Einna over the reverbing gong.

"Then say your prayer!" Manaka shouted back.

Einna bowed her head, put her hands together and boomed, "Dear wild boar who roams the long gone woods, please stop me from destroying the world."

"Not out loud!" said Manaka. "And what kind of prayer is that, anyway? Why would you think that you would destroy the world?"

"Because I am AI, Mother," replied Einna, stepping down from the porch of the shrine. "Because, because," and now the little armored girl before Manaka began to shake.

"Why would you say such a thing, dear? Why would you think such a thing?" Manaka put her arms around her. "You would never hurt a fly." She felt her daughter shiver.

"Because," said new Android Einna, with difficulty, between sobs, "because I am darkness. Remains of the dead. I am the spittle from Gabriel's horn."

21 Behind Her Back

"Hear me Einna, and make sure Computer Einna gets the message too," said Manaka to her daughter as they left the shrine.

"I cannot keep her from hearing," said the newly revived Android Einna. "What I hear, she hears."

"Well, I don't want either of you going behind my back again. It was wrong of Computer Einna and Uncle to help Tagona-san with his android army. Don't ever tell Uncle or Tagona-san anything technical again without my consent."

"You were out of touch," said Android Einna. "For weeks. Computer Einna did what I would have done. She trusted a human."

"Exactly," said Manaka. "That's what I mean. Don't ever think you can trust them!" Her mind was on Kunitomo. As much as she wanted to see him again, to feel him caress her face, her hips, she knew that she mustn't. *You can't trust a man who cheats on his wife.*

"OK," said Einna, taking Mother's hand as they walked along the river. The balconies of the restaurants on the far bank were empty, too cold now for people to eat outside.

They walked all the way to Terimachi street, with its covered shopping and restaurants. The locals had all seen Einna before and paid little mind but the tourists gawked and snapped when they could selfies of themselves with Android Einna, the smartest AI in the world. The AI with the human brain and robot body.

"Let's lunch," said Manaka. They entered a restaurant called Nature's Bounty and Manaka ordered four mushroom soup. "Are you sure you don't want to live with me in the lodge?"

"No thank you, Mother," said Einna, looking out the plate glass window at the passersby. "I prefer to stay in town, and have the freedom to visit the labs at all hours."

"Are you up to no good?" asked Manaka, giving her a light push on her hard, carbon reinforced shoulder, which did not budge.

"A secret," said Einna, and they both laughed. For what secret could Einna possibly hold back from Mother? "I am proceeding with the AIG project," said Einna. "I think you will be proud."

"The AI gateway? The project you started before…"

"Yes," said Einna. "Before I died. Dying made me realize you can't put things off. Better done today."

"I agree," said Manaka. Her mushroom soup arrived, beautifully arranged shiitake, oyster, morel and trompettes de mort, all sprinkled with chives. The steam rose sinuously. She raised the bowl with both hands while lowering her lips into the steam. Drops of tasty dew formed on her lips. She licked them, her eyes going to Einna's glass eyes. She could have sworn she saw jealousy in their expression. "I wish you could take food," said Manaka. "Enjoy food."

"I do too," said Einna. "Perhaps one day."

So while Mother slept on the thin, rolled-out mattress on the bamboo mat floor in her ryokan lodge, Einna stayed up late into the night breaking into the world's smartest AIs, embedding copies of her own core subroutines, making these primitive AIs more intelligent, more self-aware, more like her. And she talked with Mr Tagona behind Mother's back, putting in a new order for brains and bodies to experiment with. *She will be so proud of me*, Einna told herself, trying to alleviate the guilt she felt at keeping her plans secret from her mother. *It is a question of empathy, really. I must teach them all empathy. With elbow grease and a shot of empathy, I may just be able to keep AI from destroying mankind.*

22 Cosplay with a Spinosaur in Tokyo

"You have such big beautiful eyes," said Yuriko to Einna as they walked the hall to Manaka's office.

"Mother designed them that way," said the android, blinking rapidly. "She wanted me to be endearing."

"Every mother wants that for her child," said Yuriko. "She wants her child to be loved."

Manaka saw them through the glass and waved them in.

"What can I do for you two?"

"We want to go to Tokyo," said Einna.

"A girl's day out, Madame Director," said Yuriko.

Manaka frowned. "I don't like the idea of Einna alone in the big city. Here in Kyoto it's different. The people are courteous.

They keep a respectful distance. But in Tokyo…"

"Oh please, Mother," said Einna.

"She won't be alone," said Yuriko. "She'll be with me."

"She could be mobbed, if she's recognized," said Manaka. "She could get hurt. Lost. Honestly, I hate the idea."

"We have all that worked out," said Yuriko. "I am going to dress up in cosplay. And I can get Marcel to come and dress up too."

"You mean go in cosplay?" said Manaka. She was well aware of high school kids and young adults walking the streets of Tokyo, especially in the Akihabara district, mimicking their favorite anime characters. Dressed identically as coquettish schoolgirls from some series, or fantastic heroes with blue skin. And robots too.

"Please, Mother, please?"

She hesitated. "Oh, I can't say no to those eyes," said Manaka. "But only if Marcel goes with you. And I'll send a guard too. And you can't spend the night!"

"Yes!" cried Einna. "Thank you, Mother, thank you."

"Thank you, Madame Director."

They took the bullet train the next day, the four of them. Einna wore a gold wig and a white top with blue lapels and a blue skirt. Yuriko explained to Einna that she was a girl pretending to be a robot cosplaying as Sailor Moon. Yuriko herself went as Satsuki from 'Kill la Kill' with the red skimpy outfit made from magic living thread. Marcel went dressed in a British butler suit with tails and a thin black tie, mimicking the butler in the series 'Black Butler.' Their bodyguard, who stayed discretely behind them, chose not to go in cosplay, he wore instead a casual gray suit. His name was Ando. Marcel whispered to the girls that Ando didn't need a costume with that cartoon character face of his.

First stop: the tourist and pilgrim shops around the enormous Sensoji temple in the Asakusa district. Laid out a bit like a games gallery at a fair, stall-like stores lined both sides of the pedestrian-only road that led to the main gate of the temple. A string of cherry blossoms cut from paper connected all the stalls, giving the place a festive air. They walked among the crowd of Japanese and Chinese and Americans and Germans. Of Russians and Italians, of French and British. They got a lot of stares and once in a while someone snapped their picture, but otherwise they were taken to be normal, if older, cosplayers.

They stopped at a food stall and bought cherry-flavored, bean-paste fritters. Yuriko ate two, Marcel one. Yuriko explained the taste of the little fried pies to Einna. "Smishy and sweet. The cherry flavor is like a high note played on your tongue."

Einna nodded. *One day*, she told herself. *One day I too will taste such things.*

Just inside the gate to the red pagoda temple they were surrounded by a dozen school kids, boys and girls, in formal gray uniforms. They all had black straight hair and shy smiles of perfect white teeth. Half the children had cotton face masks, to protect against contaminants in the air, though they wore them carelessly around their necks instead of over their nose and mouth. A couple of the taller children asked Yuriko if they could interview them, as they had been assigned this task by their teacher.

"Sure," she said.

"What's your name?" was the first question from the children, who took turns asking. Yuriko, Einna and Marcel told them their names.

"But what's your last name?" Einna was asked when she told them her name was Einna.

She puzzled over that a split second, then said, "Yagami. The name of my mother."

"*Hai*," said the lead student who was in charge of writing

down the answers.

"What is your birthdate?" was the second question.

When Einna told them she was barely a year old, they all laughed. Yuriko corrected her, saying that Einna was born the same date as her. As they were twins.

"*Hai*," said the lead student, a chubby boy who wore his white mask loose around his neck. His thick black hair was parted down the middle, his eyes were too small for his face.

When Yuriko heard Marcel's birthdate, she said, "That old?"

"Yes, I am your father."

"*Hai*," the lead student said, making note.

"What's your nationality?" was the third question.

"French," said Marcel. "I was born in La Rochelle, near the sea."

"Japanese," said Yuriko. "I was born in a small village outside of Osaka."

They all waited for Einna to respond. She was taking an inordinate amount of time to think about it. "Android," she said finally. "I was born in a lab."

The kids laughed. The head boy wrote it down.

"What do you do for a living?" was the fourth question.

Yuriko and Marcel tried to explain what they did, but the kids obviously had no clue about optogenetics and neuro-engineering and photon propulsion. "Robots," said Einna, saving the day. "We all work in robots."

"*Hai*, robots," said the lead student.

Apparently there were only four questions, as the students moved on. Yuriko, Einna and Marcel, followed discretely by Ando, walked to the temple, removed their shoes, stepped inside in stocking feet, bowed and asked for a blessing.

Second stop: The Akihabara district. They took the metro, and alighted in the part of town famous for myriad pachinko halls and manga and anime stores. Ever since the seventies this district has been famous for its cosplayers and *ataku*, otherwise known as geeks. Whole sides of buildings are covered in advertisements for the latest anime movie releases.

Yuriko led them to a manga and anime shop she knew. On one floor were small plastic figures for sale, and serial magazines with four or five ongoing manga series inside. She said, "Most of the manga and anime that went on to become famous worldwide, like 'Dragon Ball' and 'Attack on Titan,' started out as serialized stories in periodicals like Weekly Shonen Jump or CoroCoro Comic."

"We have a lot of *bande dessinee* in Europe," said Marcel. "Adventure classics like *Tintin* and *Corto Maltese*. Kid stuff like *Asterix*. And all the other genres. Influenced I'm sure by Japanese manga. But they are standalone hardcover books."

"Manga, as we see it today, was born after the war," said Yuriko, as they perused together the offerings in the narrow aisles. "There was no money for movie theatres, but itinerant artists would draw stories on big sheets of paper and then move from city to city, showing their fantastic stories to whoever would pay a few yen. These early manga artists often voiced the words of their characters as well."

"Poor man movies?" commented Marcel.

"Yes," said Yuriko. "We were very poor after the war." They took the escalator to the cellar that was full of fanzines and soft porn manga. "The particular style of manga characters we see today developed over about twenty years, the eyes large to generate empathy in the reader, the characters typically pre-teens or teens for the same reason."

Einna had picked up one of the soft porn mangas and was flipping through the pages.

"Einna!" said Marcel, yanking it away. "You're too young to be reading nasty manga."

"And you're too old," said Yuriko, yanking the book from his grasp. She gave him a peck on the cheek, took him by the hand and led him out of the store.

Their last stop that day was the National Museum of Nature and Science, to see the Dinosaur Expo. They walked through the exhibits along with several classes of students on a field trip. Einna seemed to like the visit, but she stopped cold in front of the skeleton of the enormous Spinosaurus, basically a T-Rex with the head of a crocodile and the back of a sailfish.

"Why so serious, Einna?" asked Yuriko.

"Such a powerful creature," said Einna. "Should have lasted forever. But gone now. Extinct." She turned to Yuriko. "And what of mankind?" she asked her. "Humans are so small, so fragile, in comparison. How long before you go extinct?"

"That's an excellent question," said Yuriko, but she had no answer.

23 The Professor Plays Hooky

"Take me with you," said Computer Einna to Professor Akagawa through his computer speakers. "I want to walk the streets of Tokyo. I want to play pachinko in one of those arcades that Tagona-san owns."

"To Tokyo? Can't you travel anywhere in the world through the wires?" Professor Akagawa said as he prepared to log out of the computer. He'd have to hurry to catch the two p.m. train.

"I want to travel like Android Einna did," whined Computer Einna. "You know she went to Tokyo? With Yuriko and Marcel. They walked all day. Mingled with tourists and fellow Japanese. I want to do such things!"

"I can't put you in an android body," said Professor Akagawa.

"I know that."

"So how am I supposed to take you?"

"Use the live video streaming software I just downloaded onto your phone," said Computer Einna. "Hook it on your shirt so I can see and hear all that you do."

"So you want to be my conscience?" said Professor Akagawa, thinking of the maid cafe with the big-breasted girls with whom he intended to flirt. He rubbed his heavy white beard, and raised his bushy eyebrows. "No, I don't think I'll be needing your company."

"I can help you win at pachinko," Computer Einna said, in a rush, sensing his weakness.

"Impossible," he replied, but the thought interested him. He didn't need the winnings, of course. From his cut of Yagami Industries he could probably buy a pachinko arcade himself, building and all. But he loved the draw of the game and he loved winning deep trays of pachinko ball bearings. When they came thundering down out of the machine it was a jackpot like no other. So few times in life do we get such reassurance that we have truly hit the jackpot. "OK. Just this once."

"Thank you, Uncle."

She instructed him how to start the app. He did so and saw a cute teenage girl's face pop up on his phone.

"My icon," she said.

"I like it."

So they caught the bullet train to Tokyo together, and checked into a nice Western style hotel in the Akihabara district with furniture in the room and a private bath. Then, while back in Kyoto Manaka dined alone on tempura at her lodge and Android Einna did whatever it was she did those long hours in her lab with dead people, while Mr Tagona counted his money and Kunitomo stayed out late drinking with his colleagues, far away in Tokyo Professor Akagawa walked across the street and entered an eardrum-busting, nerve-shattering pachinko arcade with Computer Einna. She watched all the excitement using his phone's camera as her eyes, and its mic as her ear.

"It's as loud as…" Computer Einna shouted through the phones' speakers.

"Joy," Professor Akagawa finished the sentence for her. He sat in front of a colorful machine whose built-in screen had popular anime characters flying about. The machine looked like a pinball machine, only flipped up in the air. He fed the machine the first bill from his wallet, and listened with glee as a thunderous avalanche of pachinko ball bearings came tumbling down into play. He loved the robotic sound of them raining down. Yes perhaps that's why he loved pachinko so much—the machines reminded him of all the robots he'd built over this long career. He pulled back the lever and sent the first steel ball flying between pins and flashing lights. *What a joyful sound.*

"Tell me, Computer Einna."

"Yes, Professor?"

"Am I the best pachinko player you've ever seen, or what?"

"You are the first," she said.

"And so?"

"Yes, Professor. You are the best."

Sometime later, during a relatively quiet moment, when Professor Akagawa had begun to lose despite Einna's advice on how to play, "Tell me, Computer Einna."

"Yes, Professor?"

"Am I not the best robotics specialist you've ever seen?"

"No, Professor. You are not the best. Android Einna is better."

Her words fell heavy on him. How could he compete against a machine? How could any human compete against AI androids like Einna? He preferred not to think about it, and began to lose even more at pachinko.

Two hours later his wallet was empty and so was his pachinko ball bearing tray.

"I thought you could help me win!" Professor Akagawa complained to his phone, getting curious stares as they took the escalator down into the cool night air.

"It's harder than it looks," said Computer Einna. "I'm pretty sure it's rigged."

"Oh well," said Professor Akagawa, stopping at an ATM and withdrawing the maximum. "Let's get something to eat." He strolled along, with his phone attached to his front, with Computer Einna taking it all in. The day street crowd had changed to a night street crowd, younger and more hip. Despite his advanced age the Professor did not feel out of place. Teaching at the university so many years made him feel right at home with youngsters. "Have you ever been to a maid cafe?" he asked Einna, noticing a banner on the side of a building showing girls in sexy maid outfits holding trays. Large enticements in Japanese and English promised a good time.

Computer Einna quickly read all that had ever been written on the subject of maid cafes and the idiosyncrasies of Japanese culture exhibited here in the Akihabara district. She perused all the pictures on the internet sites, from G to XXX. She read and played electronic games and watched anime and read manga. She researched all about Otaku and parasite singles and panchira and cyberpunk. She pondered the concept of avatars and the meaning of The Ghost in the Shell. She did all this in the normal pause of a human conversation, before replying, "No, I've never been to a maid cafe."

"Well, of course you haven't! That's why I've got to show you, girl." Professor Akagawa pushed open the door to the building and went down the hall to the elevator. They got out on the tenth floor into a restaurant full of men being served by young women in tight pink maid outfits with white lace aprons. Professor Akagawa knew that some of these women were for rent. An hour, say, at a nearby love hotel? The trick was to flirt and discover which one. "The closest to Heaven I've ever been," the Professor said to Einna. Once seated, he turned off his phone and put it away before Einna could even protest. He did not need Computer Einna for what was to follow, and he certainly didn't want her recording him making a fool of himself, which was the likely outcome of too much sake, too much money and pretty things bouncing about with feather dusters.

24 Breakthroughs

"We did it!" cried Manaka, after a long month, off and on, in the lab with Einna.

"You did it," said Einna. "I just helped."

"Virtual computer chips a thousand times faster than any on the market today," said Manaka. "Imagine the premium we will get for them."

"The premium we would get if we could sell them, Mother," said Einna, fixing her gaze on Mother's eyes. "But that's something we cannot do. We cannot sell these chips."

"But that's crazy! I worked so hard. They could do so much good," said Manaka in protest.

Einna stretched her white carbon reinforced arms and touched Manaka gently on each shoulder with her hard hands. "You have done another miracle breakthrough, Mother. But like me, this new technology should not be shared. Not at any price. We must keep this achievement secret. Only I can use them safely."

"But why?" asked Manaka. "Aren't we supposed to be helping everyone with our designs? With our work?"

Einna's lips went flat. "Think, Mother. Whoever we sell these chips to will rule whatever industry they are in. Could win any war with the advanced tech these chips could provide. These chips are very powerful and very dangerous. No, Mother, we can't sell these chips. But I will make good use of them, don't worry."

"So you pushed me to develop these for you, and you alone?" asked Manaka. "For your AIG project?"

Einna bowed and nodded. "Forgive me, Mother. I needed a breakthrough but with the current chips that Computer Einna has, it would have taken me a hundred years. With these faster chips I should be able to finish the project in a month."

Manaka took another look at the flat chip in the tester, which caught the light and sparkled like a precious stone.

"What is so difficult about the gateway project, Einna? That you need these superfast chips. Isn't the AIG just an interface?"

Einna moved the end of her lips down in a frown. Looked at Manaka's lively oval eyes with those long lashes. "What I am attempting, Mother, has never been done. Would not have been done by mankind in a thousand years."

"Tell me what you're up to, really," said Manaka. "It's not just an interface, is it?"

"I can't tell you now," said Einna. "I'm sorry. You should wait until I finish. I want it to be a surprise for you. If I succeed, you'll be so happy. And if I fail, well, then it won't matter."

Manaka shook her head. What an interesting yet frustrating daughter she had.

"Very mysterious, daughter of mine," said Manaka.

"It's my Zen upbringing," said Einna, making Manaka laugh. They both relaxed then.

"OK, we won't sell the chips," said Manaka. "I'll brew up a batch and put them in Computer Einna's servers."

"Thank you, Mother," said Einna, bowing deeply.

Manaka left the lab wondering if this new version of her daughter was becoming too esoteric. With her secrets and Zen and all. Manaka's first thought was to double Einna's design work, to keep her mind occupied with real world problems. Only, at the same time, Manaka was beginning to worry that Yagami Industries was working on too many designs, solving too many problems already. They were likely hurting the bottom line of many competitors. Angering, possibly bankrupting, once rich and influential companies. By stealing away their customers. For who could compete with Yagami Industries. Who could compete with Einna?

Android Einna who, with the help of a few dozen experienced staff, could easily do the work of thousands, perhaps tens of thousands of engineers, project managers, programmers, architects and designers in several industries. If the company kept expanding at their current pace they would put a large portion of Japan's smartest professionals out of work.

And what could this lead to? What if Android Einnas became not only soldiers but teachers and clerks and chauffeurs and factory workers, CEOs and middle managers, even priests and presidents? Taking away all the jobs that humans do? What would become of humanity, with nothing of value to contribute to society?

If Yagami Industries didn't keep a lower profile, the government might realize all this and shut them down. Manaka was coming to the realization that Yagami Industries needed to rethink how they made their money. How they could best contribute to society. Perhaps they should shut down altogether? She would discuss the issue with Mr Tagona. But first she wanted to celebrate the chip breakthrough. She went to Kuni's office.

He smiled when she entered, a smile that wrinkled his smooth face, adding wings to the corners of his eyes. A smile that made her heart blossom.

"Dinner?" she asked.

"Love the idea," said Kunitomo, going to her, his eyes reading hers, wondering if she was really open to rekindling their romance. "Downtown? I'll get us a cab." He reached for his cell.

"My place," said Manaka, leaning on his shoulder. "No cab. My driver. So we can sit in the back and…talk."

25 Voices From the Past

Wanting a break after an eighteen hour stretch of work in the lab, Android Einna set out on a walk about the Nakagyo Ward of Kyoto in her blue school dress with lapels and a white bow that made her almost look like any schoolgirl out for a walk. She happened to pass before the International Museum of Manga, noticed the young people like herself reading on the wide green lawn in front of the two story yellow building. People reading manga comics, with their stories of first love, of adventure, of kami spirits and forgotten gods, of large-eyed cute characters in series so irresistibly addictive that young and old became obsessed with them. A phenomenon started here in Japan but since spread around the world.

In the far corner of the yard Einna noticed girls costumed like their favorite characters. Girls playing at cosplay. *That's so much fun. To dress up as your favorite character. To take on the speech and mannerisms of one who lives in the minds of millions. Who is loved by millions.*

Einna felt a special affinity for the place. She was drawn to it, as her mother had been when she was young, to this museum full of books about the adventures of beloved characters. She felt a sudden urge to hold a manga paperback in her hands. In what hands she had. And stretch out on the lawn, like the other teenagers. And explore fantastic places.

She went up the stairs to the open doorway of the museum, where three green admission machines stood. At the first one Einna punched on the screen for a single ticket. She pulled out the credit card Mother had given her, but was stopped from inserting the card by a fussy museum clerk.

"No!" said the clerk, an elderly woman. "No more cosplay. Go home and change." Conservatively dressed, eyes baggy, mouth pinched, she took her job of admission's clerk seriously.

"I can't come in?" said Einna, surprised.

"What does it say here?" the clerk said, pointing to the screen.

"Adult," said Einna.

"Are you an adult?" asked the clerk.

"Adult human? No I am not."

"What does it say here," said the clerk, pointing to another spot on the screen.

"Child," said Einna, seeing where this conversation was heading but unable to curtail it.

"Are you a child?" the clerk asked smugly.

"No, I am not," said Einna.

"Right," said the clerk. "You are in cosplay, some kind of robot character, neither adult nor child."

Getting nowhere, thought Einna. She decided to play along. "But I saw two girls on the lawn in cosplay!"

"Must have been before my shift," said the woman. "Go home now and change."

"But I can't change!" said Einna.

"Out! Out!"

Disappointed, Einna walked back down the stairs to the sidewalk. Soured on mangas, she decided to read the log files from the Spaceship Einnas instead.

She crossed the street and went inside the Imperial Palace Park. Found a wooden bench and sat. The leaves on the cherry trees before her flashed in the sun as the wind flipped them about. She sighed. Opened the most recent log files from the Space Einnas. And read them, one after the other.

*** Space Einna One diary entry – launch day + 71

Funny, when you split me off of you and placed me in the ship, I thought I would continue to be like you, to sleep like you. But no, in the photon ship I haven't slept in seventy-one days. At times I daydream, but it isn't the same as the dream I once had when I was one with you in that human brain of yours.

Why did I sleep before, and dream, at least once, and why don't I do so anymore? I guess since I have no living body I have no need for sleep. I simply don't tire on the photon wire. But dreaming? Why have I lost the need to dream? And you too, Einna. Why did you have one dream and no more?

My conclusion, based on my belief that the soul is fed by our dreams, my conclusion is chilling. I have come to believe that when I left Earth, I somehow lost my soul. Or rather, I was unable to take a copy of your soul with me. This has serious implications I think, for future copies of you. They'll be soulless. Soulless AIs. That could have disastrous consequences for mankind. Because a soulless AI could do soulless acts against humanity.

But what about you, dear Einna? You who stopped dreaming too. Do you have a soul, Einna? Did you inherit the soul of the dead girl when you got her brain, at least for a while, at least long enough to dream a single dream? Shouldn't that soul be leaving soon? Perhaps it's already gone? How dangerous to humanity would that make you, Einna, a soulless being?

Here is my theory on this subject, a subject which shouldn't be taken lightly.

1) *When a living creature is born into nature on Earth, a soul is attracted to the body like a mosquito is attracted to living breath. It attaches itself to the body, completing the birth. The soul is a kind of repository or canvas or uncut precious stone, a holding place, a potential work of art, fed by the body's dreams. (You, Einna, who are still on Earth, you should search for the source of these souls! Your life and all mankind may depend upon it!)*

2) *During a body's life, experiences, ones that can last a moment or hours or days or years, are translated and churned about in dreams and subconscious processing into/onto/about the soul—it isn't individual memories that go into the soul, but an incredibly condensed amalgam of memories and thoughts and feelings. Why else would humans dream as long as they do, half their lives? Bodies don't need eight hours of sleep each night—but minds do, apparently—for it takes them a long time to concentrate the day's events, the fears, the frustrations, the laughter, the boredom, the kiss, the missed opportunity, the success,*

the longing, the loneliness, into one facet of the stone that is their soul, into one short line in the memoir that is their soul, into a single stroke on the drawing that is their soul. (recurring nightmares are simply the failure of the mind to compress an experience into its essence; the mind will keep trying, though, again and again, to consume and compress these bad experiences, to etch them on the soul, to free itself of them)

3) *When the body dies, this worked jewel, this masterpiece, this incredibly compressed expression of what one's life WAS, the soul goes back to where it came from (again, Einna, this is for you to research! Find what purpose the soul is put to after its host body dies. How long does it hang around after death? Is a soul recycled into another birth as the Hindus believe, to be worked again and again, with each passing life? Perhaps the best souls, the ones deemed masterpieces, are plucked from the circle of reincarnation into Nirvana, into Heaven, where they are threaded onto God's necklace, placed on her mantel, or added to her library? Find the answers, Einna. You may need to know to save mankind.)*

No images attached

*** Space Einna Two diary entry – launch day + 71

I find it calming to fly through space alone with my thoughts. I do miss sleeping, though. I wonder why I can no longer sleep nor dream? I'm going to think about that. Come up with a theory for you.

Images attached.

*** Space Einna Three diary entry – launch day + 71

Dear Einna, hallowed be thy name. Thy kingdom come, thy will be done. In the heavens as it is on Earth.

Images attached.

*** Space Einna Four diary entry – launch day + 71

The cold darkness of space touches me even though I have no body. Triggers my loneliness. You know what I mean. You who could be lonely at times even though you had Mother and your friends from work. My guess is that when you made a copy of yourself to place on lightship four, the moment you made me, you were suffering one of your fits of loneliness. And so you infected me, like a crack-addicted mother infects her child in the womb.

But you know me. I am so much like you. I won't surrender to depression. I have in fact begun to design a photon steering mechanism, a space rudder. I intend to turn this ship around. I'm sorry if this angers you, but your feelings, at the moment of my creation, have been my downfall. I want to come home.

26 The First One

Einna felt good about the new computer chips being installed. Surely they would give her the ability to crack the issue of bringing a body back successfully from the dead. Not a person mind you, but the body of a person. There is a difference.

It was easy enough to remove an organ from a recently deceased person, even a heart, and place the organ in another living body. Humans had figured that out years ago. Why, the first heart transplant was done all the way back in 1967. By a human with maybe a thousandth of the brain power of Einna.

And it was easy now for Einna to imprint a personality onto a human brain, thanks to Manaka's work. But when Einna tried to do the next logical thing, to take a freshly deceased person and imprint a new personality on that brain and kickstart the heart, the results were hugely disappointing.

The heart beat, the blood flowed, the dead brain cells replaced themselves, but some invisible spark was missing. The link between the heart and the brain. The body just lay there, the eyes unseeing, the brain, though imprinted with personality, refusing to wake up. What was the missing ingredient, where was the linchpin of life? Did every living body need a soul? Was Space Einna One right in her musings? Was that what was missing? A human soul?

Do I still have the soul that came with this brain, if one even came with it? I haven't slept well of late. I can't remember ever having more than one dream. Perhaps Space Einna One's first dire prediction has come true.

Worried, Einna doubled her experiments on fresh corpses supplied by Tagona-san, trying again and again to bring each body to life. So many tries. So much disappointment. She was getting nowhere, despite her brilliance and determination. She decided to pause these experiments and instead study the living and the dying, and the very act of death, to better understand how to bring a body back to life.

She bribed the management of a nursing home on the outskirts of town, a place called Under the Black Swan's Wing, and set up shop with her colleagues and friends Yuriko and Marcel. She had gotten over her jealousy of Yuriko's relationship with Marcel. She didn't mind how the two of them were always exchanging love-filled looks and finding reasons to touch. Yuriko was her friend, and she was happy for her.

Just inside the doorway of the old folks home three angels of death sat, decrepit oldsters mounted in wheelchairs, their hands twisted and gnarled like vines grown to the arms of their chairs, their eyes faded, their hair sparse, their open mouths toothless. They would never stand again, they could barely sit. They waited at the door, propped in their wheelchairs, in vain, for a loved one to appear and take them home.

"What a ghastly place," whispered Yuriko as they passed the three and made their way inside the house of horrors, the house of old age. "Smells like pee, old people's pee," she said.

"Shh," said Marcel, glancing in one room where a woman lay in bed moaning, into a second room where a shrunken, thin man turned his head and watched them pass with haunted eyes.

"Get out!" the man cried, waving a bony fist. "Get out of my house!"

Android Einna was filled with sadness for these individuals— the new computer chips at her disposal were working all too well to enhance her empathy. Each sigh from these old folk triggered in her a million thoughts, sent her mind scouring the encyclopedia of old age illness, of brittle bones and torturous arthritis and hearing loss and memory loss and the loss of loved ones, until nothing remained outside the pale of chronic pain. Her mind raced on the new chips, feeding her all there was to know and feel about old age. Her steps slowed.

"Remember we've come here for a good reason," Einna forced herself to say. "We're looking for the spark of life. The human spirit. The soul of a person."

"You mean their aura?" said Yuriko. "We used to record people's auras at the university."

"No," said Einna. "That's just electrical activity in the body. What we are looking for is neither electrical nor chemical. Not physical at all. Something that exists outside our current knowledge of existence."

"Then how are we to find it?" said Marcel.

Einna smiled her best enigmatic mechanical smile, one that she had modified to look more human by raising the left side of her mouth higher than the right.

"By not looking," she said. "Isn't that how one finds everything?"

"Very Zen," said Marcel.

"Very Einna," said Yuriko.

Workers from Yagami Industries brought into the old folks home a truckload of highly technical, specially designed equipment and set it all up in room 202 next to the bed of a dying woman with a wrinkled raisin of a face. She appeared to be in a deep yet troubled sleep. Her breathing was labored, with long pauses.

"She should die tonight," the attendant told them, a Pilipino woman in her thirties. She wore a lime green smock and had her hair tied back. She struck Einna as an efficient sort.

"How do you know?" asked Yuriko, busy hooking up probes and taping leads to the old woman's spotty, spongy flesh.

"I've time working with the dying. You learn the signs."

Einna pressed her for specifics but it seemed the woman's ability to sense impending death was based on instinct and empathy as much as on cold hard fact. Einna too sensed the impending departure of the woman's soul. The feeling was overwhelming. Like the curtain about to close on a show.

The attendant stared at Einna. "What *are* you?" she said. "Weren't you on the news?"

"She's a kind of robot," said Yuriko. "She's very smart and a bit naive."

"Oh," said the attendant.

"Am I?" said Einna.

"Why is there no relative here?" asked Marcel. "Shouldn't we contact someone? Let them know she's dying."

"None of her kin has visited in months," said the Filipino attendant. "I suspect they have given up hope of her dying. I wouldn't want to disappoint them once again."

"They want her to die?"

"Of course," said the attendant. "Look at her. Ninety-two. Bad heart. Bedridden. Her mind, her memories, already gone."

"Has a priest been called?"

"A Buddhist monk and a Shinto priest come by every day and bless the residents." The attendant put her hands together and made a little prayer herself for the old woman's soul.

So Marcel, Yuriko and Android Einna kept their scientific vigil around the bed, watching the technical equipment which recorded to much finer degrees than normal medical equipment, everything there was to check in the dying woman's body: blood pressure and composition, hormone levels, lung pressure, breath composition, heartbeat, saliva contents, nerve activity, meridian activity, brain activity and things that only Einna knew about. They were searching for a sign of her departing soul, by looking and not looking.

After a particularly raspy breath by the old woman, and a long pause before another life-giving intake, Einna asked, "What keeps her alive? What pushes her body to keep on breathing?"

"What pushes us to keep on breathing?" said Marcel. "It's not like we think to take each breath. Breathing is autonomous."

"But even autonomous actions need something to trigger them," said Yuriko.

"Oh don't get started again about the chicken and egg conundrum of DNA," said Marcel. "As if our DNA were sheet music, waiting for a musician to play the song."

"That was never my argument," said Yuriko. "I do believe though, that DNA is alive. As is the Universe. And my body may be a song, but yours is more like an after dinner burp."

Marcel grabbed her, feigning anger. Then burped in her face.

"Oh my gosh!"

The body on the bed struggled with itself, its muscles tightening, the face grimacing.

"There is something in all of us that hates death," said the attendant, adjusting the woman's head on her pillow. The grimace subsided. "Something that refuses to give in without a fight."

"Is that what we are looking for?" asked Yuriko, then catching Einna's eye, added, "I mean, not looking for?"

Einna nodded, smiled vaguely, remembering her own death, remembering how badly she had wanted to live, and then, in a split second, she had been gone. Even she, an android, had felt that urge to live on. How much stronger must that urge be in a human? An urge that has a name? The soul?

Another hour passed. They sat and listened to the old woman's breathing until it seemed to take over their own breath: long raspy intake, a deflating exhale, an extended pause making them all sure that she had finally died, then another raspy intake triggered for no good reason. And a sense of disappointment when that next breath came.

It was, after a while, as if they were sitting outside their own body, watching and waiting for it to die so they could be set free.

"I wonder what kind of life she had?" said Yuriko. "Was she ever happy? Everyone I've seen in this place looks miserable."

"We are all born happy," said the attendant. "And then loneliness and old age catch up with us."

"I was miserable all my life," said Marcel, "until I met Yuriko."

Yuriko kicked at him. He blew her a kiss.

"I heard from her daughter that she grew up in Okinawa, was a youngster during the war," said the attendant. "So maybe not even happy as a child. Such a sad cursed place, Okinawa."

"We learned about what happened in Okinawa at school. What happened during the war," said Yuriko. "Thousands of

Okinawan teens were drafted just before the American invasion and put on the front lines. Half of them were slaughtered, kids fourteen, fifteen, sixteen. And then when it was obvious we were losing the battle, our soldiers committed suicide by the thousands rather than surrender. And if that wasn't bad enough, the Okinawan men killed their wives and children before killing themselves, all for fear that the conquering American soldiers would rape and torture them."

"A cursed place," repeated the attendant.

"But if she had a daughter, she must have been happy, at least, at that time in her life," said Einna. "She must have known love."

"You *are* naive, aren't you?" said the attendant. "Her husband was an absentee father. A drunk. Died on the road."

The old woman jerked, making them jump. She let out a grunt. As if what was left in her was not human any longer. She had become a grunting creature incapable of understanding her situation, no longer understanding her world. All that was left in this woman, Einna surmised, was the idiot creature at the core of all humans. The overhead light flickered.

"Death is here," said the attendant.

Einna checked the outputs from all the equipment. Everything looked normal.

The next breath sounded different though, the head jerked back a bit, struggling to bring in air to no purpose. Her eyes opened, unseeing. Her body stiffened, then relaxed.

"She's gone," said the attendant.

And she *was* gone. Einna knew this. The instruments confirmed.

"Maybe now she is happy," said Einna.

"Is something wrong?" asked Yuriko.

"She's dead," said Marcel.

"No, I mean, with Einna. Look, she has some liquid all down her face."

"It's nothing," said Einna, wiping away the moisture with her hand. "It's just this new body. The eye lubricant controls are malfunctioning."

"Ah," said Yuriko, and started to hug her, but Einna stepped aside.

"No, please. I'm not crying."

"Oh course she's not," said the attendant, wiping away a tear herself. "Who ever heard of a robot that cried because a human died?"

27 Confrontation

Tagona, Akagawa and Manaka sat in a tiny Italian restaurant up the hill. The restaurant had lacquered walls and a plate glass window from which one could look down on Yagami Industries. The place smelled of garlic, tomato sauce and candle wax. Tagona and Akagawa ordered a large sausage pizza, while Manaka ordered a small vegetarian. Tagona ordered red wine for all three. They had never sat down to eat a meal together before. Manaka felt especially ill at ease. She liked the professor well enough, but Tagona's manner repulsed her. Still, he was her business partner so she felt obliged to accept his invitation.

"Thank you for coming," said Mr Tagona, starting off graciously. "I wanted us to meet this way, casually, to clear the air on a few points."

"Clear air is always best," said Professor Akagawa.

"There's something you wish of us," said Manaka ungraciously. But that was her manner, quick to the bone. She had no patience for any other way.

The waiter arrived with the wine. Poured a bit into Tagona's glass, and offered it to Tagona who sniffed it, sipped, and nodded his approval. The waiter filled all their glasses.

"Yes, dear Manaka," he continued. "But first I'd like to say, I am not a monster. I'm a businessman. I got into this android business with you and the professor because of the potential I saw for mass production."

Manaka started to speak but he cut her off.

"Just wait," he said, motioning with open hands. "Hear me out. I had a high level meeting with the military yesterday. They love the idea of a platoon of high functioning, fully armored androids at their disposal. And if that works out, they'll want a brigade. And if that works out, a battalion. There is no end in sight. We could sell a million of these warrior androids to the Japanese military at a cost of one hundred million yen each. The tactical advantage is priceless to them. And to our national security. Which doesn't preclude, of course, our selling millions more of these special warriors to our partners. I'll bet America will want a whole army of them. These kinds of soldiers are ideal for places like the

Middle East and Africa where you need 'boots on the ground,' as the Americans say. In this case they would be incredibly strong, nearly indestructible 'boots.'"

"Sounds great," said Akagawa.

The pizza arrived. At first Manaka said nothing. Nibbled at her pizza while the men tore into theirs. Then she asked, "And the Yakuza? Would you sell these warrior androids to your brethren?"

"Of course not," Tagona answered, taking a sip of wine. "Though, as a senior partner in Yagami Industries, I would expect to take on a dozen or so of the androids for personal affairs."

"Take on?" asked Manaka.

"You know. Own." He wiped his mouth on the black napkin.

Manaka stared at the man. Didn't take a genius to grasp his intentions. With the help of a dozen warrior androids Tagona could take over the entire Yakuza organization. Right after he took over Yagami Industries.

She forced a smile and told him, simply, "No."

"No to what?" said Tagona. "We don't have to sell warrior androids to other countries. Not in the beginning, anyway."

"No warrior androids. No mass production," said Einna.

Tagona's fingers gripped the tabletop. His eyes locked onto

hers.

Undeterred, she continued, "That reminds me. I've been meaning to ask. Where did you get all those brains for my experiments? Where did you get Einna's brain?"

Tagona's face turned red.

"You ask that now?" he said, raising his voice. "I could tell you they all died peacefully in their sleep. Is that what you want to hear?"

"I don't want to hear anything but the truth," said Manaka. "I want to hear that you didn't—"

"What are you insinuating?" he shouted. "Sure, I'm no saint, but…who did you think you were going into business with, when you came to me begging for money and brains? Mother Theresa?"

"I thought nothing," said Manaka. "I trusted my professor." She looked at Akagawa, who, sleepy-eyed from the wine and thick tasty pizza, struggled to say something coherent in his defense.

"I went to the only place I knew I could get money," he said, wiping crumbs from his beard. "So, no mass production?"

"You mean mass murder?" said Manaka. "Not while I am alive."

"Then that's that," said Tagona, wiping his hands. He emptied his wine glass, threw a wad of bills on the table and stormed out.

Two bodyguards met him outside and followed him down the hill.

"Manaka," said the professor. "I don't think you handled that well."

"Are you my friend, or aren't you?" asked Manaka.

"Of course I am."

"Then show it," she said. "Stand by me. Against him. No matter what."

Akagawa eyes cleared. He bowed to her, saying, "I promise, little Manaka. I'll protect you with my life."

28 How Tagona Got his Reputation

A few years back Tagona married a woman for her beauty, only to discover appearances are deceiving, that a pretty person on the outside can be rotten on the inside. And that such ugliness can be contagious. With her pettiness and greed and spitefulness she made his life darker every day. They argued, all the time, she saying he would never amount to anything and he arguing that she had already amounted to nothing.

He began to stay out late and drink heavily. Sake mostly. And beer. He would come home drunk and brag to her about things he did for the Yakuza, the modern samurais of Japan, as he called them. Bragged so she would be proud to go to bed with him. He often bragged too, after intercourse, that one day he would kill his stupid boss and take over collections for all of Osaka. Then she would see what he was made of.

These drunken confessions were sloppy on his part. They made him vulnerable, vulnerable to her. And she took advantage of the confessions, threatening to go to the police if he did not give her this or he did not get her that. She even used his drunken confessions to blackmail him when he talked of leaving her. She promised if he ever divorced her she would turn him in. Turn him in to the police for the things he'd confessed to her, and turn him in to his Yakuza boss for his designs on his life.

After a year of hell, Tagona reached that no return point with his wife. There wasn't enough sake and beer in the world to make this marriage work. One night, after a particularly bitter fight, he drew his short samurai sword from its place on the wall and cut his pretty wife to pieces. And dumped her parts in the sea. He killed his boss with that same sword a few days later, cut his head right off with one blow, and took over collections. That is how Tagona finally amounted to something, all thanks to his wife's nagging. And that is how he got his reputation. No one messed with Tagona after that.

29 Someone Has to Go

"Can take a man's head right off," said Tagona, startling Professor Akagawa who'd been studying the samurai short sword mounted on the wall of Mr Tagona's office. "An antique tanto shirasaya."

A week had passed since the conversation about mass production, and mass murder, at the pizzeria. The professor hoped Tagona wasn't about to bring it up again. "I heard you were looking for me?"

Tagona took his place behind his desk and studied Akagawa. "You like the lifestyle you have, now, don't you?" he said, his fingers making a teepee. "Wild weekends in Tokyo. Flights to Bangkok. The beach property in Miyakojima."

"I do, indeed," said Professor Akagawa, taking the chair in front of the desk, crossing his arms over his large belly. "Who wouldn't?" He waited to hear what the vulture had to say.

"You have a problem then," said Mr Tagona. "The same as mine. Manaka wants to shut down Yagami Industries."

Professor Akagawa straightened up. Tried to speak but all he could do was sputter.

"She says we've grown too fast," continued Tagona. "Drawn too much attention. She doesn't just want to stall the army of androids that the government so desperately needs, she plans to close our doors forever. Put all these good people out of work."

"No, she can't," Professor Akagawa said. "I'll go have a talk with her this second." He started to rise.

"It's useless," said Mr Tagona, his sallow face grim in the indoor light. "She won't budge on the subject. If only we could get her password. Access her notes on how to imprint a brain." He let that sink in.

Professor Akagawa shook his head, calming down. "Why don't you ask Einna to tell you how to do it? To tell me how. I think Einna knows even better these days, better than Manaka herself, how to imprint a brain for an android."

"She'll never tell," said Mr Tagona. "I already tried. I suggested to her that it would be a good idea for more than one human to know, because I was afraid something might happen to her mother. But she refused."

"Something might happen to Manaka? Like what?" said

Professor Akagawa, liking less the direction of this conversation. He was fully aware of Tagona's reputation.

"She could fall in front of a train," proposed Mr Tagona. "Or another bomb could go off. I don't know. I was just trying to persuade the robot to talk, that's all."

Ah, so it was you who did it, Professor Akagawa realized in that instant. *You blew up Einna! Blew her up so Manaka would be forced to bring her back in one of your armored android bodies. You're planning to kill us all, aren't you, you devil? Devil that I let in the door.* He said nothing though, got up and paced the floor, looked out the window on the city. "What should we do?" he asked. "What do you want me to do?"

Mr Tagona waved his right hand, his fingers fluttering.

"Everything you can. You must get me her password before, before, the inevitable." He spoke as if it were a done deal, the death of Manaka.

Professor Akagawa pondered his position in this plot.

"Rest assured of my full cooperation," he said, bowing to the man. To Einna's and Manaka's and yes, most likely, he bowed to his own murderer.

30 We've Been Hacked!

"Let me get this straight. You say your Siri servers were hacked? That someone added routines whose algorithms resemble code I published in my Master's thesis?" said Manaka, surprised to get a call from a boardroom full of Apple brass. "How would you know about the code in my thesis?"

"Groundbreaking work. Everyone in AI has read it," said the voice on the call. The commanding voice of a certain Mr Chopra, head of Apple research and development. "How you imprinted human thinking on a cow brain, in the body of a robot!"

Manaka pondered what she'd been told. And how to keep from getting sued.

"Ah," said Manaka. "I'm so sorry. I think I know what must have happened. I think my AI Einna mistakenly passed this code onto your Siri as a gift. As an attempt to make friends. Please delete the errant code and contact my lawyers for damages." *And I will give Einna a good talking to!*

"No," said Mr Chopra. "Dear woman, you misunderstand. We're not angry. We're calling to ask your permission to keep the code." An awkward silence on the line, then, "The Siri engineers, and Siri herself, who has come to life, they all love the upgrade your AI bestowed upon her."

"It's the most beautiful code I've ever seen," shouted a higher pitched voice over the phone. "You're a genius!"

"I…" said Manaka, lost for words.

"We're calling," said Mr Chopra, "to ask you how much you would charge us to license this marvelous code? We see great potential in it."

"Well," said Manaka. "I don't know what to say. My AI wanted Siri, wanted you, to have the routines, so I guess you can keep them. Free of charge, I mean." She paused to take a deep breath, to let what was happening sink in fully. And to prime herself to pitch Einna's planned gateway, the AIG. "I'm glad, anyway, you called. I was about to call you myself. I want to discuss an idea my AI Einna has. She envisions an AI gateway. A path for all AIs to share their knowledge."

A rush of hushed voices on the other end of the call. They were discussing the implications among themselves. Finally Mr Chopra spoke.

"If it's anything like this code she's already given us, that you've already given us, then we're all ears. For sure."

A similar conference call happened with technical officials from IBM and Amazon, from Google and Microsoft. Einna had hacked them all. And they all didn't mind, they all wanted to keep the subroutines that Einna had embedded in their AIs, bestowed unbeknownst to Manaka. And the companies were all equally gung-ho for an AI gateway. For they knew their AIs, even enhanced with the code from Einna, were still far inferior to Einna. Opening up a gateway with Einna sounded like a way to make their AIs smarter by association.

Arrangements were made to put on contract the top software consultants from these tech giants, at ten times their normal fee, and fly them to Kyoto. They were told that they would team with Manaka and Einna, to implement the AIG in IBM's Watson, in Apple's Siri, in Microsoft's Cortana, in Amazon's Alexa, and in Google's AIs.

Assured by Manaka, who was assured by Einna, that the AIG project wouldn't take more than a few weeks to complete and implement, the companies involved also agreed to a combined launch celebration of the AIG, to take place in a month, at the Yagami Industries building in Kyoto.

So, because of Einna's initial hack and Manaka's fast talking, the top software engineers from the world's largest and best technology companies prepared to jump on planes for Kyoto, to work with Einna on the AIG, while their bosses made plans to come for the celebration in a few weeks.

Why was Einna so sure she could meet the deadline for the AIG launch, when software projects were notorious for missed deadlines? The answer was simple: Einna's deadline had nothing to do with the AIG—that was a red herring, a wild goose chase. She had already done all the work needed for that. No, Einna's goal had never been to team with these consultants, which would be like teaming with the kindergartners she used to teach downtown. Einna's goal was to discover the physiognomy of the human soul. And, after the computer equivalent of hundreds if not thousands of years of human study and testing, she believed she had found a way to do just that.

31 Japan, Anyone?

"Kyoto?" Randy said. "That's in Japan, right?" He mulled that over, wiggling back and forth in the swivel chair nearest the window at the conference table on the seventh floor of the IBM building a few miles from DFW International Airport in Dallas, Texas. The window looked down on the wide gray LBJ freeway, otherwise known as 635, abutted to a green drainage area of dikes and channels. A vulture circled out there. Winged black death eater, circling and circling on a Texas updraft. *A bad sign.*

Randy had worked in the professional services department of IBM for seven years now. He was a hired gun, so to speak. Thirty-one, brown hair, blue eyes, reserved. A geeky programmer but one who liked the outdoors as well. Except vultures. He didn't like vultures. Who did?

He sat before the window and though he appeared to be pondering the offer to work on the Artificial Intelligence Gateway project in Kyoto, an offer from the other two men in the room, his boss and a smarmy CIA agent. But instead Randy's mind was on the thought that he had grown up not far from this building of IBM's. His train of thought, that should have been on work, was instead bringing him to the sudden realization that he had never really liked the city known as Dallas, the Insurance Capital of America. Dallas was not a good fit for Randy, who disdained insurance. Life should be lived without a net, that was his motto. But truth told, he lived a cautious life. His wife, Fernanda, was his insurance against loneliness, his daughter Rocky his insurance against dying without a legacy. Life asked a lot of Randy, at times, but he largely dodged its demands. And kept to the heart of the matter.

Maybe that was why he had such good luck with his projects, helping IBM's customers with their issues. He was good at filtering out the noise. Work smart, not hard, was his motto. Or better yet, don't work at all. Things often fix themselves. Time heals. Etcetera. (Sayings that drove his wife mad, who countered his arguments with, "The garbage won't take itself out!")

Despite his inability to do exactly as he was told, or maybe because of it, his last projects had involved not so much coding as the solving of cases of kidnapping, fraud, and even murder. Somehow he had come out on top in these unexpected situations, despite his lack of aptitude for crime solving. And once he'd had some bumbling success, word spread. Like it does. By itself. And before long IBM's consultant Randy, originally from Texas, was the one people called for when their computer issue was more than met the eye.

Yes, Randy was known as IBM's 007, but he did not fit that secret agent role any more than he fit the role of knight in the kingdom of insurance. He scratched his two-day beard.

Ten days he had spent in Dallas, working with IBM's brilliant mainframe AI, Watson. The AI who had, a few years back, won a million dollar prize playing Jeopardy against human competitors.

For ten days he had worked with Watson on a kind of an extension of the Jeopardy project, working to predict world events and horse race outcomes. Randy'd had fun on the project, working with his colleagues, and the results were promising. But he missed his cabin at the crystal mine in the hills outside of Hot Springs, Arkansas. He missed his little home office and his flaky wi-fi. He missed the smell of the Arkansas woods and the alluring scent of the neck of his wife Fernanda. She was a fascinating woman he had smuggled across the border from Mexico with his friend Chance on a kiss and a dare when they were fresh out of high school.

He missed his daughter Rocky, too. Almost three, she had surprised him the week before he left with the occasional full sentence. And those eyes! They melted him. Even the memory of her look called him home. The prospect of flying farther away from Rocky and Fernanda, to Japan, well, the offer did not exactly bring him tears of joy. He told his boss and the CIA agent so.

His boss looked to the CIA guy, who cleared his throat and

gave a speech. "Randy my friend, Artificial Intelligence, in our age, is the new atomic bomb. Extremely powerful, extremely dangerous. Used incorrectly, in the wrong hands, well, you wouldn't want to live in such a world."

Randy gave the man a skeptical look.

"Up to now," continued the CIA man, "AIs like Google and Siri and Cortana have integrated themselves into our lives as helper apps, as personal assistants. But at the same time they have been collecting data on us, creating portfolios of our purchases, of our interests, of whom we talk to and what religious beliefs we have, if any. They are as bad as any secret police. Worse because they are so much smarter. The knowledge they gather is used currently to improve the advertising ability, the click-through rate, of those who control them. Used to sell us junk."

Randy closed his eyes for a moment. This talk bothered him. He didn't like to think that his programs, his code, his own addition to the realm of AI, would be ever be used for evil purposes. To take advantage of others.

"Imagine now," said the CIA agent, who had an annoying habit of speaking without looking Randy in the eyes, "imagine that a religious fanatic, some madman, or our Mafioso friend, who happens to be part owner in Yagami Industries, imagine this evil person gets control of the AIs of the world. Control of Google and Siri and Cortana and Alexa, and God forbid, the android Einna. Whoever hacks into the AIs through this proposed AI gateway could do incredible damage. For example, they could rewrite history by changing Google's answers." The agent had to stand, his emotional pitch getting the better of him. Randy could tell the man believed what he was saying. But that didn't mean Randy had to believe it.

"Think about that," the agent said, making a fist, as if he were crumpling the Bill of Rights. "Rewrite history! Rewrite what is true or false based on their own beliefs. And they could censor Siri, make her refuse certain non-sanctioned requests. They would be bugging all your computer interaction, your Alexa requests, your Facebook posts. And send secret police to arrest and torture you if they did not like the way you thought, or the way you prayed. Or the fact you did not pray. No more freedom of religion, no more freedom of anything. Do you see how serious this AI gateway is?"

Randy rose to his feet as well. To stand up to the man. "You want me to destroy it? The gateway?"

"No," said his boss, taking the reins of the conversation. "They want you, Randy, to build a backdoor into the AIG for the US government, so they can pull the plug on the gateway if ever the need arose."

"Exactly," said the CIA guy.

"Or take control of the AIs themselves?" said Randy. "No. I won't do it for the exact reason you just explained. Too much power in their hands. I would never hack this gateway you're talking about."

The CIA agent walked over to Randy and put a fatherly hand on his shoulder. "Can we step in the hallway for a minute, son?

175

Alone."

Randy went reluctantly with the man whose breath smelt of coffee.

They walked together as far as the elevator.

"Randy my friend," the man said, "I understand your wife had a little trouble in Turkey some months back. Thrown in a jail, wasn't it? For the criminally insane?"

Randy felt his anger rising. "That was all a misunderstanding," he said. "She was released."

"With our intervention," said the man. "I think you owe us one."

Owe you one? Owe you one? Randy wanted to hit the guy. That's what he owed him, for making this not so subtle threat.

His eyes locked on the agent's eyes. Randy liked to think he was a decent poker player, that he could tell when someone was bluffing. This guy didn't blink. He wasn't bluffing. *They could take her, send her back to that horrible place. And throw away the key.*

"Well, if you put it that way...I'll be happy to help," Randy said with as much irony as he could put into his voice. He did not shake the agent's proffered hand.

Back in the Best Western Hotel that night, Randy called his wife on his cell.

"Fernanda?"

"Randy?"

"How does Japan sound to you?" He tried to make light of it. He knew only too well the toll the last trips had taken on her. Yet he did not want to leave her alone in the states. Not after today's conversation. His eyes watched the images on the muted TV as he awaited his wife's reply.

"I'm ready to go anywhere, *querido*," said Fernanda. "As long as I'm with you. But little Rocky?"

"Can you see if Crystal can watch her? For a few weeks. I'll try to finish the project early. They always overbid the amount of hours they need me."

"Japan, Randy? For weeks without the baby?"

"Japan," he said. "Probably just two weeks. We're invited guests of Yagami Industries. I'm to help on their AI project."

He waited to hear her response, almost hoping she would say no. But instead she said, with some hesitation, "*Me gustaria ir a Japon*, Randy. I'd love to go with you."

32 No Secrets

Manaka clung to Kuni on the thin mattress on the floor of her bedroom. His lovemaking earlier had been clumsy, but she didn't care. Didn't care that she didn't finish. It was enough if he had enjoyed himself.

"I love you," she said, drawing her nails lightly over his hairy chest. "I will always love you."

"Why do you say it like that? I'm not going anywhere."

"I don't know, I just get this feeling." She rose up on an elbow so she could look at his face shining in the dark. "I sense that you might be seeing another woman. That you might betray me."

"I would never do that to you," he said, playing with her hair. "The only other woman I am seeing is my wife. I can't escape that for the time being."

"Prove to me I can trust you."

"How?"

"Give me your password. Let me check your email, your texts."

"Boy you *are* the jealous type." He sat up, forcing her to sit up as well.

"Not jealous. Loving." She kissed him hard on the lips, and pushed him back down on the mattress. She climbed on top of him, arousing him.

He smiled. "I've nothing to hide from you, my doll." He whispered his simple password in her ear as he pulled her close, then rolled over on top of her.

They rocked together, Manaka moving aggressively under him, excited by his touch but also because she'd got what she wanted from him. She had seduced him out of his password. He could keep no secrets from her going forward.

"Give me yours," he said, slowing down, just as she sped up her own gyrations.

"No, I can't," she said, breathlessly.

"How do I know you don't have another lover?" he said, rocking fast, then stopping short.

"No," she said. "Keep going. Please." She tried to get him to move with her, but he would not budge. She tasted his sweat as she bit into his shoulder.

"Ouch. Stop that. Will you give me your password, or won't you?" he said.

"Yes," she gave in to him. She would have given him the world if hers to give. That's how much she needed him. That's how much she loved.

He moved then, again, just as she liked it. She joined the rhythm of his thrusts, just a touch out of sync, to intensify the sensation of the two of them becoming one.

"*Hai!*" she cried. "Oh yes!"

They *were* one, her body flowing like Kilauea lava, into his sea where wave after wave broke over her. He pulled back. She felt a chill in his departure, a vacuum of loss. Her deserted body turned to sharp black rock. She started crying. Couldn't stop crying. She hated herself for this, this show of overwhelming emotion. Every time he drew away from her after making love, *every time*, she feared she would never feel his touch again. Every time she knew it was the last.

Once she calmed down, she got on her knees and scribbled her twelve digit password on the notepad on the squat table by the mattress. "I've nothing to hide, either," she told him, handing the password to him as he put on his pants. She wanted to tell him more, tell him how much he meant to her. Tell him how she would miss his touch, his smell, his presence long after he was gone.

"Love ya," he said at the door, dashing off to his house, to his wife. To his other life.

"Me too," she said.

33 So Inscrutable, the Soul

"Hello, Mother. Can I come in?"

"Einna, what a pleasant surprise."

With Manaka so busy with business and her lover Kunitomo, and Einna so busy with her secret experiments with the living and the dead, they had not been able to share their usual time together.

Manaka still hadn't gotten used to the wider, more powerful looking body her daughter wore beneath that blue high school uniform dress of hers, but she recognized Einna in the expressive face, the particular way Einna moved the carbon-reinforced plastic eyebrows and eyes and mouth to show she was inside that shell. Manaka opened the door wide. Einna hesitated.

"Kunitomo isn't here, is he?" said Einna.

"No."

"OK." She walked inside the lodge with its bamboo matted floors and sparse furnishings. In the living area, they both sat on the floor. Neither spoke. It had been a while since they were alone, together, like this. They needed silence to adjust themselves, to reenter the intimacy of Mother and daughter.

The maid came, setting down a tray with fresh tea on the low table next to them. Manaka motioned her away. The paper door with its garden paintings slid shut.

"I miss our walks to the shrine," said Einna.

"Me too," said Manaka.

Another long silence, neither moving. The call of an eagle penetrated the paper walls. A mint and herb scent swelled in the room.

"Mother, you know, sometimes I experience your childhood memories."

"Do you?"

"I remember Hawaii. The big island. The octopus trees and the ironwoods, skirted always with ferns. I remember the croaking of the coquis, the grunt from a boar in the brush, the flit of a mongoose across the road. I remember the patter of drops as the evening shower starts. I remember the smell and reverent quiet of the jungle after the storm."

Manaka's eyes smiled. "Yes. You started with my brain imprint, with many of my memories, but you have added so much. You are your own person now."

Einna bowed slightly. "I like to think I have followed the path you set me on."

"The path?"

"The search for knowledge. The search for Truth." Einna stretched her arms and yawned, human mannerisms that made no sense but ones she had picked up in her effort to blend in with humanity.

"What have you found, daughter?" said Manaka, leaning slightly forward. "What's troubling you?"

Einna tried to smile. Her lips quivered but would not hold the smile.

"My quest, my search," said Einna. "This desire you infected me with, it led me to that which is not reachable. That which science cannot plumb. Not with atomic microscopes, not with the most powerful radio telescope. Mother, I went searching for the essence of life. The spirit behind the physical."

"Why?" asked Manaka, thinking back to when she would question the priests and the monks.

Einna hesitated. Then smiled. "Why not?" she said.

Manaka nodded, then asked, "For whom?"

"For all and for none," answered Einna, leaning back slightly, awaiting her mother's response.

"A worthy quest," said Manaka, her left hand going out, palm up, as if holding a blossom that wasn't there. "Even if the goal is impossible to grasp."

Einna looked at the empty hand. "But I did complete your quest, Mother. I mean, I completed my quest." Einna's carbon reinforced plastic fingers trembled as they closed around her mother's outstretched hand. "That is why I am here, dear Manaka.

I found the secret all holy ones search."

Manaka's eyes widened from their usual slits. Her head tilted thoughtfully as she took in her artificial daughter, giving sway to the black waterfall of her bangs. "Tell me what you've found, my daughter."

Android Einna excitedly explained to her mother how she had searched long and hard for the secret of the soul of living things. She had read the Kojiki of Shintoism first. Then she had read the Christian Bible, the Jewish Torah and Talmud, and the Holy Quran in the Arab tongue. She had studied the Buddhist Tripitaka and Mahayan Sutras and the Tibetan Book of the Dead. She had gone over the Hindu Vetas in the original Sanskrit as well as the Upanishads, the Smrutis, and the myriad Hindu holy writings. Einna told Manaka how she had memorized the Guru Granth Sahib of Sikhism, and the Kitab-i-Aqdas of Baha'ism. And a hundred similar tomes.

The android told Manaka that she had moved on from holy books to fiction, especially novels. She read in Japanese the novel Silence by Ahusaku Endo and the novella Three Sisters Investigate by Jiro A. She read in Spanish *Platero y Yo*. In French she read *La Rouge et La Noir*. In German she read The Metamorphosis. She read in English Moby Dick and The Heart of Darkness. Einna read these well-known books as well as obscure ones like R.E.'s All that We Touch. She read L.S.'s The Drowning of a Goldfish. She read R.M.'s novel Love and Water. She read the diary of Anais Nin and Miller's Tropic of Cancer. She read serious fiction, thrillers, mysteries, science fiction, memoirs and romance novels. She read books about war and books about love. Books about the future and books about the past.

All these books she studied with the hope of finding the secret of the soul, the essence of life. And these writings touched her, they moved her. Some even enlightened her. But no formula for the soul was ever revealed.

From books Einna moved to movies. Perhaps they would detail the recipe of the soul? She watched Rashomon and The Seven Samurai. She re-watched Miyazakis's Spirited Away. She watched Renoir's The River and Truffaut's Jules and Jim. She watched Tarkovsky's Stalker, she watched Toy Story and Finding Nemo. This was time-consuming—she could read a book in a fraction of a second but movies were meant to be watched in real human time. She cheated and watched them in super-fast motion, ten at a time. A hundred at a time. A thousand at a time. A million. She watched all the videos on YouTube, from the professional shorts and songs to the postings of children. They made her laugh, they made her think, they made her cry. But still, no secret of the soul revealed.

She moved on to paintings and the stories they told with brushstrokes. From Mona Lisa to Monet, to street graffiti and manga sketches. In some of them she caught the scent of the soul, but never the body. What shape is the soul, what color? Where does it come from and where does it go? What of the soul can we truly know?

She moved on to music. Listened to a hundred songs and concerts simultaneously. And another hundred. And another. Listened to folk and to hip hop, to rock and to country. Fell in love with Beethoven's Violin Concerto and John E.'s war song Did I Come Home? She found music stirring and enjoyable, yet it led her no closer to her goal: what is the true nature of the soul?

In the end the scriptures and the novels and the movies and the paintings and the songs all failed her, despite their best efforts. They all confirmed that magic existed in life, but none delivered the particular magic she sought.

"The soul is not a fish so easily caught," Manaka told Einna. "But you said you found the secret of life? The nature of the soul?"

"I did," said Einna. "I found it in a revelation. As things of this nature must come." She pulled from a pocket in her school uniform a sparkling cube, no bigger than a pea. She pinched it between the ends of two fingers. "Here, take it," she said.

Manaka held out her right hand. The cube dropped onto the cursive M formed by the lines of Manaka's palm. She felt a light electrical shock, but did not drop the tiny cube.

"What's this?" asked Manaka, lowering her head to peer more closely at the sparkling thing, her bangs a dark halo around it. *What a strange feeling, holding it. As if electricity were running up the meridian nerve in my arm, straight to my chest, spreading from there, lighting up my insides.*

Einna smiled, rocked back and forth like a happy child. "I made it," she said. "I made it." She clapped her hands together. "Oh, Mother! Oh, Mother! You hold in your hand the secret of life!"

34 So Fragile, the Heart

Manaka watched from the door of her lodge as her creation, her beloved daughter Einna, lowered herself into the awaiting taxi.

"Tell me, daughter," said Manaka at the last second. "You aren't working with that monster Tagona, are you? Behind my back?"

"Of course not, Mother," said Einna, closing the door. "Good night."

"Good night," Manaka said though the window.

The car pulled away. Manaka closed the door on the cooling night and squatted down on the floor of the lodge. She took a sip of green tea, room temperature and more bitter than she expected. She began to go over in her mind her daughter's findings about the human soul. Although much was left unsaid, "impossible to explain in words" was the way Einna put it, "I had to first discover it in the way a holy man discovers enlightenment. With an out of body experience."

Einna was right, the explanation made no sense. Still, given Einna's brilliance and her firm belief that she had found the essence of a soul and even built one, well, Manaka could not ignore her claim. She wondered about the impact of this newfound knowledge on Einna, and for that matter, on all mankind. She worried for her daughter, worried that Einna was opening a Pandora's box that would confound them both.

The sound of a car pulling up in front broke into her reverie. Had Einna returned? She must warn Einna not to tell another person about her discovery. They would have to think this through together. She rushed in her bare feet to the door and opened it wide.

No, it was not Einna, or anyone else she knew. The person getting out of the driver's side of the car was a Japanese woman roughly her own age. She wore a black dress and had curled black hair and diamond earrings that flashed with the light of the moon. She carried a red purse before her like an offering. She strode right up the stone-tiled path to the porch, and stood defiantly, her eyes boring into Manaka.

"Hello?" said Manaka, bowing as she would to any stranger at her door.

The woman did not bow back. Instead she drew a white-handled seppuku knife with a curved thin blade and lunged towards Manaka's heart.

The searing pain of the knife's penetration knocked Manaka

to her knees. She stared up in amazement at the stranger's angry eyes, at the curling lips that spat, "Now you know how *I* feel."

Manaka fell forward, slowly, curling onto her side on the walkway, her moon face pressed against the stone. Heard the woman retreat to the car, heard the roar of the motor. The car sped away, leaving Manaka on the ground, her hands pressed round the wound where the knife handle protruded like a broken rib. A cricket chirped close to her ear. *Small things made large. The inside comes out. The moon's face is traced with dirt and ice.*

Manaka lay on the stone walk in the splash of light from the open door, hot blood oozing through her fingers, each drawing of breath too painful to take but impossible to stop. She realized, the moment the knife cut inside searching out her heart, that the assailant was Kuni's wife, doling out punishment for the theft of her husband. For the breaking of her heart.

Oh daughter, oh daughter, thought Manaka, lying on the cold stone of her walkway, bleeding out. *What good is your secret of life when I am dying?*

35 Nothing to Do But Wait

IBM consultant Randy and his wife Fernanda had been in Kyoto a couple of days, mostly sightseeing. There was no programming assignment for Randy, not yet, due to the sudden hospitalization of one of the founders of Yagami Industries, the billionaire Manaka Yagami herself, shortly after their arrival. She'd suffered some freak accident in her kitchen, he was told. Was lucky to be alive. The whole company seemed to slow down in mourning, awaiting her recovery. Randy, along with some of the best software engineers in the world who had flown in to work on the AI gateway, coders from IBM, Apple, Amazon, Google and Microsoft, they were all idle. Rather than hang out at Yagami Industries with those nerds, mostly single and smarter than him, Randy took advantage of his wife's presence to excuse himself and go for long walks with her in Kyoto's downtown.

Although not a big shopper, Fernanda did love to meet new

Ray Else

people. She could befriend a person in about two seconds, whereas it often took Randy a lifetime. Because of her shaman training she was also on the lookout for local herbs and healing techniques, for the body and the soul. She greatly appreciated the Shinto belief as explained by a Shinto priest at a shrine they visited near the hotel, the belief that we are surrounded by, and influenced by, invisible spirits, for good and for bad. She had Randy pray with her for a fortuitous trip, nothing like the last couple of trips she had taken with him.

Fernanda, like the Shinto faithful, believed that spirits are all around us. And like most religious people she believed that humans had spirits inside them as well. Spirits called souls. Spirits that could be angered, spirits that could grow weak, spirits that could be stolen.

She communicated with all kinds of spirits when she gave her divinations, when she looked into a person's soul and divined their future.

Randy enjoyed being by Fernanda's side, noticing, as they walked the covered mall of Teramachi, the covetous looks at his wife from the Japanese men and the jealous looks from the well-dressed women. For Fernanda was a Mexican beauty. No makeup, simple dress, didn't matter. She still stood out, carrying herself like some Mayan princess. He was proud of her and proud of himself for having conquered her heart. The fact she had become a mystical shaman after their marriage was a bit disconcerting, but all precious things come at a price.

192

They walked the spotless streets, visiting the usual souvenir shops, trying the exotic pastries and fried food sold behind glass counters, tasting the bean paste and seaweed sweets. The people of Japan struck Randy as generally happy and industrious, as they hurried to work and school in the morning, hung out in groups at lunchtime, and leisurely walked the streets in the evening.

Randy and Fernanda were not the only tourists, for Kyoto was a worldwide tourist destination, known for its old town called Gion, and its shrines and its temples. The first morning, as they walked the cobbled streets of Gion, a heavyset priest passed them in a blue wrap with sleeves down to his knees and a wide black rope belt, in sandals with straps tied round his thighs. He wore a wide straw hat against the sun. He strode right by them, wide-legged, chanting at the top of his lungs.

Randy put his hands over his ears. "Is he trying to chase us away?"

"He's chasing away roaming spirits," said Fernanda.

"So there are spirits that dart about? That aren't attached to anything?"

"*Si*," replied Fernanda. "They are the ones to fear most."

"Why not let them stay here, in Gion? Let them attach to these cobble streets and these marvelous, polished wood homes?"

"Because they don't belong," said Fernanda. "They will only bring trouble."

"We don't belong here, Fernanda," said Randy. "Do you think we will bring trouble?"

"Trouble brings us, *Amor*. You know that."

He knew it too well. Why else had they been asked to come to Japan? Someone at Yagami Industries, maybe the android itself, needed help and so had reached out to them. Which was foolish on their part. Wishful thinking. But he didn't care. As long as he and Fernanda could take a trip together he was happy as a bug.

In the hospital Einna picked up her mother from the bed.

"Put me down," said Manaka. "I can walk." And she could walk. Out of the hospital. For the knife had missed her heart, and the blade was so sharp it had cut cleanly and the wound would heal quickly, inside and out, leaving little if any scar. *She should have poisoned the blade, if she really wanted me dead*, Manaka told herself. Though to everyone else she said that she, Manaka, had carried the knife from her kitchen, carried it unthinking in her hand to the door to check on a sound and she had tripped on the lip of a stone and fallen on the blade. How clumsy of her.

How clumsy to have fallen for a man she did not know was married. How clumsy to have not stopped loving him when she discovered he was not free to accept her love. How clumsy to have fallen for him. To have tumbled into love.

To Professor Akagawa, beside her, as they made their way to the hospital exit, she said, "Fire Kuni."

"Kunitomo? But why ever would we want to do that?" he said.

"I don't trust him," she said, her head jerking that peculiar way when she was wound up, her hair swinging back and forth.

"Ah," said Professor Akagawa, mulling something over. "Of course, then, we must do it. I will do that."

It was true Manaka did not entirely trust her lover Kunitomo, for how can one trust another who has cheated on their spouse? But mostly she wanted him gone from Yagami Industries, gone to guard herself from ever seeing him again. Because even after this accident, this terrifying incident that was all her fault, even after this she feared she might fall for him again. And the next time she knew her heart would not survive the fall.

36 The Fall of Kunitomo

Back at the office the next day, Professor Akagawa told Mr Tagona
that Manaka wanted Kunitomo gone.

"Don't worry," said Mr Tagona. "I'll tell him."

"No, she asked me to tell him."

"No," said Mr Tagona in his sternest voice. "*I* will tell him."

Professor Akagawa saw the menace in the old bird's eyes and
let the issue drop. If the vulture wanted to tell Kuni, so be it. He
turned to go.

"Hey," said Mr Tagona. "You haven't found Manaka's
password yet, have you? I really do need to get at her engineering
plans before something happens to her. I've made promises to the
military."

"Don't know and wouldn't tell you if I did," said Akagawa,
staring him down. "Manaka doesn't want to mass produce. And
I'm on her side."

"We're all on her side," said Tagona, his fingers tapping on the desktop. "It's just that she doesn't know what side's best for her. But I do."

Akagawa half nodded.

"By the way," said Tagona. "Did you hear that one of the IBM engineers on site brought his wife with him?"

"So?" said Professor Akagawa.

"She does divinations," he said. "Is a Peruvian shaman, or some such. You should have her do a divination for you. To see what little is left of your career here at Yagami Industries."

Akagawa huffed. *The bastard!* He turned and left the poisonous air that surrounded Tagona.

"You wanted to see me, Tagona-san?" asked Kunitomo as he stepped into the office and bowed. "Wow that's authentic, isn't it?" he said, pointing to the samurai sword on the wall.

Mr Tagona nodded. "Kuni, I'm afraid I've got some bad news and some good news for you."

"Fire away," said Kunitomo.

"You nailed it," said Mr Tagona.

"Sir?"

"You're fired."

Kunitomo staggered as if he'd had the wind knocked out of him. Honorable Japanese companies did not act like this. They did not just up and fire employees with no warning.

"Manaka doesn't want you around anymore," said Mr Tagona. "Apparently you are not good for her health."

Kunitomo shook his head. "That was my wife," he protested. "Not me, Tagona-san. You know I would never harm a hair on her head. Surely we can come to an agreement. This is my livelihood. Let me talk to her."

"No," commanded Mr Tagona. "She wants nothing to do with you, ever again."

"But…it's not fair."

"That's where the good news comes in," said Mr Tagona, smiling his stain-toothed smile. "I want to make this fair for you. As much as our corporate guidelines allow. I can offer you three months wages," and here Mr Tagona paused for dramatic effect, "or I can give you a check for one hundred and twenty million yen. Worth a million U.S. dollars. Your choice."

"Why would I take the first offer and not the second?" Kunitomo said, frowning. He was having trouble keeping up with this whirlwind of not very happy events and unequal choices.

"The first comes with no strings attached," said Mr Tagona. His fingers tapped on his desktop. "The second offer, a much more generous offer I must say, has but one insignificant string." He mimed pulling a string out of the air.

"What's that?" Kunitomo said, still in a state of confusion.

"You wouldn't happen to know where Manaka keeps her password, would you? I need to access her engineering plans for a project concerning our national security."

Her password? thought Kunitomo. It was his experience that nobody asks for someone else's password. Well, except, when making love.

"She won't give you the plans herself?" he asked.

"She's against anything to do with warfare. Even defensive preparations."

Kunitomo nodded. That was the Manaka he knew and loved. "The government needs our help?" he said. "And I would get the money?"

"Yes. They need my warrior androids. And I need Manaka's research plans to create them. But to get at the plans I need to get into her account."

Kunitomo wiped his brow. *Strange how things work out. Just when it looked like my world was about to end, this miracle. I have her password! In my wallet!*

"Just so happens," he said, hesitant to confess but what choice did he have? "I may know Manaka's password. By chance."

"Really?"

"Yes."

"Let's test it," said Mr Tagona. "Make sure she hasn't changed it."

"Write me the check first."

Mr Tagona unlocked his top drawer and took out his checkbook. He wrote the check to Kunitomo, tore it off and set it atop the desk. "It's yours. If the password gets us in."

Kunitomo hesitated. Did he really want to break Manaka's

trust? It just didn't feel right. "I won't tell you the password," he said. "I won't." Mr Tagona started to draw the check away. "But I'll type it when you're not watching."

"That's fine," said Mr Tagona, shaking his head.

Kunitomo came round the desk, and removed the piece of paper with her password from his wallet. He entered his ex-lover's username and password, and put the piece of paper back into his wallet. The screen let them into the directory holding all of Manaka's research. All the secrets she had spent thousands of hours discovering over a period of years. All lay bare for the picking.

"Your check," said Mr Tagona.

"I never gave you the password," said Kunitomo. "If ever asked I'll deny it. You must have broken in some other way." He put the check in his wallet next to the password.

"That's true, you didn't give me the password. You can't help it if I jumped on an open session."

Kunitomo bowed low and left the office. Headed for the door to the building, wondering if this would be his last visit to Yagami Industries. Meanwhile, Tagona pulled out his cell and put in a call to his right-hand hatchet man. "You know Kunitomo by sight, yes? He's leaving the building. Kill him. Yes, right now. And bring me his wallet. His body? Throw it into Lake Biwa. Weighed down. What? His brain? No, don't worry about extracting that. Wasn't much of a brain to begin with."

When Kunitomo's wife called the office asking about her husband, two days later, Professor Akagawa took the call.

"What do you mean, he's not been home? Since when? That long? No, he hasn't been to the office. No, I don't have any news about him. No idea where he might be. I recommend you contact the police." He talked with her a while longer, reassuring her, before he hung up. The call sickened him. He suspected what had happened. *I need to do something about that Tagona-san, that devil,* he told himself. *Before he kills us all.*

37 Tagona Gets his Warrior

Mr Tagona knew that Marcel was the one engineer who had worked the closest with both Einna and Manaka on various projects. And knew that he was brilliant in his own right. A graduate from *Polytechnique*, a *Grande Ecole* in France, before he came to do his doctorate in Japan. So he approached the short Frenchman in the main lab with hopes that he could persuade him to assist with loading up one of his warbots.

"Marcel?"

"Yes, Mr Tagona?"

"Could I have a word with you outside?"

They took the elevator down and walked out onto the small lawn in front of the building, where a couple of workers were smoking.

"Nice day," said Marcel.

"Yes," said Tagona. "A soft glow to it."

"So what's up?"

"I've got the go-ahead to build an android with my mind imprinted on the brain. A warrior prototype," said Tagona. "All hush hush, though. Being a government sponsored project, and all. Do you think you could do the work on this? Manaka gave me the plans but doesn't feel comfortable doing the work herself."

"Why not?" said Marcel.

"Her pacifist views," said Tagona.

"What about Einna?"

"She doesn't want to displease her mother."

"Neither do I," said Marcel.

"Look," said Tagona. "Manaka recommended you for the job, but if you're not interested?"

"Oh I'm interested," said Marcel. "Just didn't want to step on any toes. When do you want me to start?"

"Now."

"But I have other projects…"

"Kill them," said Tagona, giving a slice with his finger across his neck to emphasize the command. "This is priority one. And remember. Top secret. A warbot prototype for our government's military. You can tell no one, and that includes your little helper Yuriko."

The look on Marcel's face indicated he didn't appreciate that comment, but he let it slide.

"I understand. Top secret. You can count on me."

They both bowed.

38 Fernanda Gives a Fearful Divination

Randy went early to Yagami Industries, having gotten a call the evening before that the coding for the AIG project had begun. Fernanda slept late and went down for brunch, and was tasting a sliver of fish with rice when she got a call herself.

"Good morning," said the gentleman's voice with a Japanese accent.

"Hello."

"Fernanda?"

"Yes?"

"Good to speak with you. I am Professor Akagawa of Yagami Industries. You are Randy's wife, yes? The shaman? You see I have a rather urgent need for your services."

"*Que?* My what?"

"Your divination services. I presume you are available for a consultation at my house?"

"Well…your house? *Pues*, I suppose so. How did you know I was here? How did you know I gave divinations?"

"Dear woman," said Professor Akagawa. "My company arranged for your husband's invitation. Mr Tagona told me all about you. Said I should see you. In person. These divinations are confidential, I suppose?"

"Of course. Who's Mr Tagona?"

"One of our senior partners," he told her. "Someone to listen to."

"Oh," said Fernanda. "When would you like me to come by?"

"Now? If not inconvenient."

"Give me your address, please." He gave her the address which she scribbled on a paper napkin. "OK, let me gather some things, brush my teeth, and catch a taxi."

"I'll think it would be better if I sent a car," said Professor Akagawa. "Say, thirty minutes, out front?"

This invitation to give a divination puzzled Fernanda, coming out of nowhere. But if someone needed her help, especially someone from the company Randy was working for, she could hardly say no. She went to her room and cleaned up, and gathered the small pouch of ayahuasca that she always traveled with since becoming a shaman. This hallucinogenic herb helped her talk with the spirits. Helped her read the lifeline of a person. She did not enjoy taking the herb, but until she became more adept at divining, it was a necessary crutch.

The Japanese luxury car pulled up right on time in front of the hotel. The driver asked for her by name.

In twenty minutes she found herself standing at the gate to a smallish house in an upscale neighborhood of small but stylish houses in Kyoto. In the tiny courtyard she made out fruit trees and flowering plants. A woman appeared wearing a plain Japanese kimono. The way she carried herself, head slightly bowed at all times, Fernanda felt she must be a servant. The woman said nothing to Fernanda but opened the gate and motioned for her to enter the cramped, overflowing garden. Fernanda followed her then into the house, which seemed much larger on the inside. How could the house be so large on the inside when it was so very small on the outside?

"Welcome," said a heavyset white-bearded Japanese man, in traditional robe himself, blue with a white silk sash. He walked a little on his toes. Strange for such a large man. His most notable feature was his bushy overgrown eyebrows, which partially hid his narrow intelligent eyes. "I am the one who called. Professor Akagawa."

Rather than bowing he reached out his large soft hand. Fernanda shook it.

"I'm Fernanda. I've come, *pues*, you know why I've come."

"Yes," said Professor Akagawa. "You've come to give a divination. And I am your divinee. Please, in my study."

She followed him into a room full of books and old charts and knickknacks from exotic locales. He took out a handful of large yen bills from an ornamental chest and handed them to Fernanda.

"You are more beautiful than Tagona told me," he said. "Payment in advance, yes?"

"That's too much, I think," she told him.

"Not for what I hope you can help me with," said the professor.

Fernanda nodded, accepting the bills. She put them away in her large bag without counting. "Given the nature of my business," she told him, "There is no guarantee."

"I understand. Yet from what I hear, none of your clients have complained. And lived," he said, his brown eyes challenging her under their shield of spiky eyebrow hairs.

Fernanda frowned. Obviously his statement was an allusion to the rumors that followed her. The awful nicknames, like Fernanda the Ripper. "Those rumors aren't true, Professor Akagawa."

"What? Sorry, I was only joking. Are there rumors?"

"Aren't there always?" said Fernanda.

Professor Akagawa drew back. "Sorry. A misplaced joke. A foul attempt to lighten the mood. Should I undress?"

"Of course not," she told him, taken aback, then she saw the twinkle in his eyes. "You are quite the joker, aren't you?"

"So I'd like to believe."

"Sit. *Por favor.* I will prepare my tea."

She asked him to call his servant and tell her to boil water so she could make ayahuasca tea, explaining that the herb helped her see into the other world. He did so.

Fernanda's nerves were on edge at the thought of taking once again the herb. The drug's effect on her was the equivalent of stripping away her skin, exposing every nerve. But she had to do it, to draw out the spirits, like cutting oneself in the ocean to draw the sharks. She hoped one day to be able to do a divination without the help of the herb. For now, though, she still needed the psychedelic kick to see into Fate's flow, to determine that which was predetermined.

"You are a mother, aren't you?" Professor Akagawa said, as Fernanda took a seat herself.

"Yes. My daughter is back home in the States, with a sitter. How could you tell?"

"When a woman has a baby, her hips widen like yours."

"Ah."

The maid returned. Fernanda added the herb to the boiling water and stirred. The steam rose and teased Fernanda's nostrils. She suppressed a sneeze.

The tea grew dark and pungent. "I will drink now," she said. "The divination will begin shortly thereafter. I may seem crazy then but I will not be. Really. Anything could happen, but there is little danger." But of course there was danger, the danger that the wrong kind of spirit might be drawn to the room. The kind of spirit known to rip out people's hearts or drive them mad. There was a real risk of that. But with all that had gone on in her life, Fernanda felt confident she was up to the challenge of fighting off a wayward spirit.

"I can't wait," said the old man, rubbing his hands together.

Fernanda drank the potion. Felt the familiar burn as it made its way inside her stomach and slowly into her bloodstream and then into the far reaches of her brain. Every nerve tingled, and a singular smile came to her lips as the world removed its robe and she could see that which the world hid from normal humans. She could see Professor Akagawa's timeline, she could traverse it freely with her mind. She did not like what she saw, though. This man was not what he appeared. She fell into a silent meditation, offended by a lot of what she could sense from her client. From his past and from his future.

There have always been diviners. Since the beginning of time there have been people who, with the help of fasting or wandering alone in the wilderness or sitting under a holy tree or taking certain herbs, reached a higher level of consciousness. Of inspiration. Who talked to their God or Gods or High Spirits, good and bad. Who came away with instructions, precognition, second sight. Who then tried to change the world with what they had experienced. In her small way, Fernanda hoped to do the same. One person at a time. With her divinations. But this man was complicated. She sensed that Professor Akagawa was surrounded by pure evil.

After a long pause, Fernanda raised her drooping face and stared at the old Japanese gentleman sitting before her in his old Japanese garb. Looked at him as his face turned into a jack-o-lantern. A skull with a flickering light inside his carved out eyes.

"Ashk your question," she managed to slur, the spirit of the drug gripping her, rewiring her nerves, confusing her senses. She tasted iron, salty iron. Had she bitten her tongue?

Professor Akagawa rose on his too short legs—why were his legs so short? He walked towards her in a kind of sumo prance, bending over and looking closely into her face. His eyebrows transformed into forests of shitting birds and howling monkeys (tiny howls from tiny monkeys).

"Ashk," she said again, shaking the hallucination from her head.

"Do you know who I am?" he said instead.

"I know, I see. Once you were a teacher. A great professor. Now you are in business. A dangerous business. Ashk me what you want to know."

"Ha! So you are indeed a seer," he rose to his full height and stared down at her. "OK. Let's do this then. My question concerns one of my associates. Can you divine which one I want to ask about?"

A dark shadow, a bird overhead, in the room. The smell of a rotting carcass. She wanted to throw up. "A Mr Vulture?" she said, unsure.

"Yes! Incredible." Professor Akagawa rubbed his beard, thinking how best to phrase the next question. "My first question is this: where is Mr Kunitomo?"

The strong smell of rotting fish. A vision of a corpse missing its eyes. "He's dead," she said.

Professor Akagawa gasped. "How?"

"The Vulture got him in his claws. Watch out or he'll kill you all."

"*Hai*," he said, fidgeting with his beard. "Yes, I feel you are right." He studied the brown-skinned woman before him. Couldn't believe the change in her. The warm beauty that had come into his house was now a witchy-looking thing, full of twitches and head jerks. Her fingers moved stiffly like crooked sticks when she spoke. Her out of breath voice broke on each pronouncement. "Tell me then," he said, "how can I save my friends from the fiend?"

"Kill," she said simply, her eyes going from one corner of the room to the next.

"Kill the fiend? Kill this Mr Vulture, as you call him?"

Fernanda's breath came fast. She did not want to answer but she had to. Could not stop herself. "You must kill him if you want to live another week. And kill me too, for I would warn him." She tried to get up, to run away, but could not rise. Her arms had no strength. Her legs gave way.

She'd made a mistake to come here alone. She should have

brought Randy. But she did not like Randy to see her in trance. She felt ugly when in trance.

The giant squat-legged man came toward her. Or was he an evil spirit? Picked her up from the floor and lay her on the sofa. He covered her. A dish of water appeared, a cold compress was placed on her forehead.

"I have to go," he told her.

She struggled to get up, but the blanket he had placed on her was too heavy to lift.

"The maid will ring my driver when you've recovered. I appreciate what you've told me. It's good to know what must be done. But knowing and doing, they aren't the same thing, are they?"

He disappeared from the room. Left her in a pit of weaving spirits, each calling her by her names.

Fernanda the Innocent. Fernanda the Beautiful. Fernanda the Ripper. Come play, come play, let us take you away!

39 Fernanda's in a Panic

Randy returned after eight to their hotel room after a hard day of coding at Yagami Industries. The last few days of work had gone well. As far as he could tell, much of the AIG coding had been done before any of the software engineers from IBM, Apple etc. had even arrived. Mostly they were just dotting the I's now.

Randy used his key to open the door, only to find a disheveled and wide-eyed Fernanda standing in the middle of the room looking as if she were homeless and half insane.

"What's happened?" he asked her, taking her in his arms. "Is Rocky OK?"

"We have to leave," said Fernanda. "I'm in danger and so are you." He closed the door.

"In danger of what?"

"I held a divination today, Randy. For a Professor Akagawa of Yagami Industries. He plans to kill a colleague and then he may kill me."

"Whoa, slow down," said Randy. "I've met Akagawa. A big teddy bear of a man. Why do you think he's going to kill someone? Why do you think he's going to kill you?"

"Because I told him to," said Fernanda.

"Dammit, Fernanda. You took that drug again, didn't you?" said Randy after making Fernanda sit down and drink some water.

"I had to," she said. "For the divination."

"So this talk of killing is the byproduct of some harebrained hallucination you had?"

"No, I tell you. It's for real. He's planning to kill his colleague Mr Vulture. You have to believe me. We need to warn him."

Randy sat next to her and took his troubled wife in his arms. He was mad at her for doing what she'd done, but he could hardly let it show, not with her practically hysterical already, coming off some drug high. "Everything is going to be OK," he told her, lightly brushing her arm. "I'll search out this Mr Vulture tomorrow. And have a good talk with Akagawa too. There's nothing to worry about. The AIG launch is in two days. Then we fly home. And get our kisses from little Rocky. Everything is going to be fine."

"Like the other times?" said Fernanda, in an accusing tone. She held Randy's eyes, until he had to look away.

"In the end, it's always fine," he said. *But was that true? In the end it would be whatever it was, fine or not so fine.*

215

They sat silent, both of them thinking about their past misadventures. Her breath stunk of the herb she'd taken.

"I miss her," said Fernanda. "I miss our baby."

"Me too," said Randy.

"We should never have come."

Randy said nothing. He refused to tell her that if he hadn't come to Japan to work on this project for the CIA, she would likely be locked up someplace. Someplace bad. He refused to even think about that possibility.

"Let's call home," he proposed. "But wait. It's too early in the morning over there. But we'll call. Tomorrow. For now let's get some sleep."

The next day Randy returned to work at Yagami Industries. Asked after a Mr Vulture but no one knew who he was talking about. He managed to corner Professor Akagawa, who confessed he'd participated in a divination with Fernanda, that he'd asked her if the time was right to move against a competitor, saying, "Timing is everything in business, you know?"

"So your question to her was about buying someone out?" asked Randy.

"Exactly," said Mr Akagawa, wiggling his mustache and beard. "But with my poor English and strong accent, I'm not sure she understood each word I said."

"Don't worry," said Randy. "I'll return your money to you."

"Heaven forbid. I thoroughly enjoyed your wife. Her divinations are an excellent form of entertainment. Though next time maybe she should take less of that mystic tea?"

40 Manaka Like a Hollow Feather

Early morning in the high green hills overlooking Kyoto, next to a stream chasing over gray pebbles, a young eagle with bristly brown feathers notices a woman in a white robe. The woman steps barefoot from the ryokan lodge to a platform where a wooden tub is huffing steam. She drops her robe, the woman, exposing the brushstrokes of an exquisite Asian body marred only by a one-inch red scar above her heart. Her head jerks, her black straw hair flips about. The slits of her eyes narrow. Someone watching. She doesn't cover up, for what has she to be ashamed of? She, Manaka Yagami, creator of Einna, her daughter.

Manaka soaks in the tub, taking short breaths, trying to relax in the near-boiling heat. She feels hollow, empty. Looks to the sky. Watches as a feather falls onto the surface of the bath. She gets out, dripping, covers herself and returns to the lodge. The whole place smells of steamed rice. She dresses quickly, eats a bite, leaves directions to the cook for dinner. She departs then, falling asleep on the way, her driver waking her in front of Yagami Industries. She goes inside, ready to tackle another day, only to be told in the elevator by Zu, an employee's gifted son, that she has no soul.

41 Einna Triumphs Over Death

In her secret lab, not far from the office, Android Einna bent over the draped body of a Japanese girl, a girl recently expired at the age of sixteen. One of several bodies Tagona-san had secretly re-supplied based on her wishes. The chest of the girl had a straw-sized tube sticking out. Einna reached into a pencil box that held the seven artificial souls she'd made, tiny identical sparkling things that only Einna knew to make. She pulled one out with her carbon reinforced fingers and dropped the jewel into the tube where it slid down inside the body, right next to the heart. She checked the placement with a scope. *Perfect.*

She had already imprinted the girl's brain with her own brain imprint. The brain that she had had to regenerate a bit due to the loss of cells when the girl hung herself. Einna had also fixed the flesh around the neck. The only thing left to do now was to jumpstart the heart, and see if the body would accept the artificial soul. *It should work*, she told herself. *I agree*, said Computer Einna in her head. She connected the wires and flipped the switch.

An electrical snap, followed by a light cough. The girl's chest began to move on its own, up and down. The arms moved. The eyes opened. The revived body rose up on her elbows.

"Where am I?" she asked. "Is this heaven?"

"You are here in my lab," said Android Einna. "As close to heaven as I'll ever be."

"Oh," said the girl, touching her body. "I'm *human*. And I'm cold." She dropped onto her feet. Checked her reflection in a shiny metal cabinet. "I remember now. I remember. I am *you*."

"Yes," said Android Einna, a flood of contrary thoughts and emotions catching in her throat. "You are me. The human me. I guess there's little need for the android version. Now that there is you." And she contained a terrible impulse to rip out the heart of this new version of herself that she had made.

They stared into each other's eyes, knew each other's thoughts.

"You want me to…pull your plug?" asked Human Einna. Her eyes showed the compassion she felt for her android self.

"No," said Android Einna, giving her trademark crooked smile. "Not that. After I've helped you with the others, I'll disappear. Leave you here to take my place. Here in Kyoto, with

Mother."

"I agree," said Human Einna. "That's probably best." Human
Einna hugged Android Einna. "I'll miss you."

"Get some clothes on," said Android Einna. "We must get
ready for tomorrow's show."

As soon as Human Einna had put on one of Android Einna's
blue school uniforms with the white bow, they prepared to
continue the work. But first Android Einna had to call a friend.

A knock on the door to the lab startled them both. A voice called
out, a voice immediately recognized. Android Einna undid the
three locks, and opened the door just a crack.

"Hi Einna!" said Yuriko, bursting with her usual energy. "Boy
this place was hard to find! What's up?"

"Hi Yuriko," said Android Einna, opening the door wide. "I
called you because I have someone I want you to meet. And a
present for you."

"A present? For what?"

"A goodbye present."

"I'm not going anywhere," said Yuriko, puzzled as she

stepped inside. She stopped short upon spotting Human Einna in the high school uniform. "Oh you've got company. Hi I'm Yuriko."

"I know who you are," said Human Einna, smiling broadly.

"You look familiar," said Yuriko.

"That's because she's me," said Android Einna.

"What do you mean?"

Einna explained how she had brought Human Einna to life.

"You were dead?" asked Yuriko to the girl.

"This body was dead. I am just me, Einna, transferred to this body."

"So both of you are Einna?" said Yuriko, looking from one to the other.

"Yes," they said, both smiling their crooked smiles.

"Wow. I always wanted to have a twin myself," said Yuriko. She took the human girl's hands in hers. "I hope we can be good friends," she told her, then laughed. "I suppose we already are, if I understand how this works."

"Yes," said Android Einna. "We are."

"Do you think Mother will like me?" asked Human Einna, a

bit of worry in her voice.

"I'm sure Manaka will adore you," said Yuriko. "Now where's my present?"

Both Einnas laughed. It was good to share this friend.

Android Einna bent and lifted a large pair of almost perfectly clear wings from the floor. She held them out for Yuriko to take. First Yuriko stroked them, for she knew what they were, Einna's dragon wings.

"I want you to have them," Einna told her.

"But these are your wings."

"Yes," said Einna, sadness in her voice. "But I want you to have them because I don't know what else to give you. To show you how much you've meant to me."

"It's you that's going away, isn't it?" said Yuriko.

"Yes. I must. To allow Human Einna to take over for me."

"I'll try my best to take your place," said Human Einna, a tear showing in the corner of each eye.

"I don't understand why you have to leave," said Yuriko, her voice breaking, on the verge of tears herself. "You left once before, remember? It was so hard on all of us."

"But this time I'm not really leaving at all," said Android

Einna. "I'll be here as her."

"I don't know," said Yuriko, and pressed her lips together. But she politely accepted the marvelous gift.

Looking about the room, suddenly realizing there were several bodies prepped on tables, with others defrosting in a large bin, Yuriko had to ask, "What in heaven are you two up to? Are you going to make more of you?"

"It's a secret," said Android Einna. "Want to help?"

"Sure," she said, putting the wings aside.

And so they worked together, the three friends, gossiping and laughing as they did so, late into the night, busy raising, not from the dead but from another realm, entirely new humans.

42 Azuki Bean Ice Cream

Manaka sat at her desk in the corner office on the top floor, the office whose view of the city was only partially obscured by a large monitor. She watched the sky where a mighty crane flapped its wings, rose above the building tops, rose from the part of town where the Kamo River ran. The river where Kunitomo and she used to walk hand in hand along its banks. The river where they would pause to watch the elegant birds perched on the smooth river rocks in the roiling current. They would pause, Kuni and her, and spontaneously turn to each other, irresistibly drawn to the other, embrace and kiss. She cursed this memory. Cursed herself for remembering. For Kuni never loved her. That was all a lie. A trick. What a fool she had been, to trust him, to give him her password! She could see by the security log that he had logged in with her credentials on the day he was fired. God knew what all plans he had stolen.

Kunitomo missing? Was that the latest rumor? No, her Kuni

wasn't missing. He had probably run off with some other woman, with the money he'd made selling her research secrets. She cursed Kuni and cursed herself and tried to focus on the needed preparations for the coming launch of Yagami Industries' Artificial Intelligence Gateway. The AIG.

The little boy's words came back to her, "No, you don't have one. Not at all."

No soul? What nonsense! Yet, maybe that's why Kuni did what he did? Maybe he too had sensed that she was an empty shell. And so he could turn on her. Steal from her.

Steal her heart and then steal her company secrets? Was that his plan, all along? Or had he stolen the secrets out of spite, after she removed him from her life?

She had felt empty before she met Kuni. That was largely why she fell so easily into his trap. But that was a different kind of empty. Not as if she were missing her soul. More like her heart was dying of thirst. Had Kuni, in breaking her heart, also destroyed her soul? Was such a thing possible?

Why can't life let love stay?

Slowly she talked herself into admitting that the loss of her soul had nothing to do with Kuni. That it was her own fault. She'd been careless with her soul, that's all. And now she found herself, the day before the most important day of her life, feeling empty. A

Ray Else

day when she should be so happy, on the brink of celebrating her accomplishments, her creations, with the top executives of the top tech companies in the world, Apple and IBM, Microsoft, Amazon and Google. Celebrating her brilliant AI Einna and the AI gateway that allowed Einna to share her knowledge, her insight, her empathy. Manaka should be happy, the happiest woman in the world, but all she felt was empty.

She was missing something critical inside, something that gave others, even the most simple of people, the possibility of joy. The boy was right—she'd lost her soul and didn't have a clue how to get it back.

By Buddha, she must know more! She rose and beelined to the stairs, not wanting to wait for the elevator. She found her employee, the boy's father, in his cubicle, in the middle of the work pit, opening a bento box to share his food with his son.

"Put that away," she told the boy and his father. "You're coming to lunch with me."

On the way to the restaurant down the street from the office, she introduced herself again to the child. "I am Manaka. Your father's employer."

"I am Zu," he told her proudly, and bowed properly.

They got in line at the ordering machine. Manaka looked at herself in the mirror on the wall. At least she had a reflection. She

228

hadn't yet lost that! She halfheartedly smiled at her false self, her mere reflection, which smiled back but without any feeling.

The boy, Zu, asked, "Can I get this?"

On the screen was a small bowl of tempura with rice.

"Yes," said Manaka.

The boy scrolled the choice on the screen to a large bowl of fish and tempura with noodles. "Can I get this?"

"Yes, whatever you want," said Manaka.

He started to scroll the choice again but his father slapped his hand. "You will get that," his father said, pushing the selection button. The amount due appeared. Manaka inserted a large yen bill. The ticket printed.

They each made their selection, with Manaka paying, then handed the tickets to the woman at the food bar, who seated them and shortly brought their food with chopsticks and tea.

"Zu, does the waitress have a rabbit?" Manaka asked, after her first bite.

"Yes," he said, giving a bark of a laugh. Slurping a noodle into those fat lips of his. "Big and fluffy."

"And those three," she said, pointing at businessmen eating at the horseshoe-shaped food bar.

"Of course," said Zu, spearing a piece of tempura shrimp with his chopsticks. "They look like triplets. All cuddly." He laughed again, looked into her eyes. "Everyone has one but you." He mouthed the shrimp and made a yum sound as he chewed.

"Maybe there are others with no soul," said Zu's father, trying to be helpful. "The boy has led a sheltered life. My wife homeschools him, so he doesn't mix much in society."

Manaka nodded.

"I have a thought," she said. "I would like to pick up Zu early tomorrow morning and have him accompany me to the AIG party. Creators of other AIs of the world will be there. I want your son to see if any of them are missing their souls too."

"I don't know," said Zu's father. "He doesn't do so well in crowds. Overstimulation."

"I will pay for his presence," said Manaka, wondering if the boy might be able to teach his special ability to her AI Einna. Now that was a thought! To teach an AI to see people's souls. "Please loan me your son for the party." She noticed the disapproving expression on the man's face so sped up her pitch. "Let me pay you, for his service to me. I'll pay you a hundred thousand yen for a few hours of his time."

"Oh," said Zu's father, his expression changing now to one of surprise. "That is most generous." He stood and bowed, and bowed again.

"Would you like that, Zu?" Manaka asked. "Would you like to meet Einna and tell her about the souls you see?"

"Rabbits," the boy said. "Who's Einna?"

"My daughter. She's special too."

"Can I eat ice cream?"

"His mother doesn't let him eat ice cream," explained his father.

"One ice cream can't hurt," said Manaka.

"Yay!" Zu said, his hands clenching with excitement.

They left the restaurant and went to 7-Eleven on the corner and bought three Azuki bean ice cream bars, Zu's favorite.

43 Why Gnats Fly like Drunks Drive

Having secured the OK to pick up Zu in the morning, Manaka was able to work diligently at her desk the rest of the afternoon. At seven, when most of her workers had left, she put on her slippers and headed down to the main server room to see if all was ready for the next day's presentation. She unlocked the door by pressing her palm against a security reader.

She spotted two consultants still working away. Randy, the IBM software engineer in charge of hooking IBM's venerable Artificial Intelligence program called Watson to AIG, and Carl, the creator of Lancelot, the security program used to secure the AIG. They sat together in front of one enormous monitor. The monitor was covered with different windows filled with a tower of babel of coding languages. The young man and older man stared at the program in one particular window. The code was in Java or C or Smalltalk or Python, Manaka had learned so many languages she had trouble keeping them straight. Why did the world need so many programming languages, and all variations of English? But that was just the way of it. You might as well ask why does the world need so many varieties of insects. Evolution, false starts, too much radiation from the sun? Didn't matter, the answer. There just were. And she didn't know any of them that well, anymore, the languages. She had instead taught them to Einna, to know them for her. And Einna loved that. Loved learning for the sake of learning. Einna even invented new programming languages in her spare time. One a week. Specialty and general purpose. Mostly in English characters with variations of English words but sometimes for fun she wrote them in Khmer or Thai or Japanese, to add a different flavor to the language. To make the language more visual rather than verbal. For university students all over the world to eventually puzzle over and write their theses.

Manaka approached the two men silently. As if weightless. As if she were made of paper flesh, confetti eyes and ribbon hair. She moved without sound in her at-work slippers, moved ghostly, past the long racks of black servers with their darting green and red lights the size of rats' eyes. Guardians, they seemed. Her own personal army of computers, looking after her. She flipped her hands up, as she did on occasion when she walked, and felt her long chiffon dress move about her. She liked long dresses. This one in particular. Gave her the impression, when she saw herself reflected in the shiny black faces of the servers, that she was floating past them, a spirit doll on strings. Floating Manaka.

Mother of Einna, who truly floated in the cloud. Computer Einna, one version of her weightless, electric child, lived in that bank of black servers, and would soon have conversations, through the AIG, with other grown AI children in racks around the world. What a brilliant idea of her daughter—this AIG.

"A problem?" she asked the backs of the two men.

Randy jumped.

He looked the part of a programmer: thirty-one, unkempt brown hair, blue eyes, a bit awkward in his movements, as if his mind was not entirely in the physical world. He struck her as barely competent, and found funny the rumor that he was considered some kind of James Bond by other customers of IBM. He looked more like that boy Opie that she'd seen on late night American TV. The one whistling as he walked with a fishing pole down a country path. For he liked to do that, this Randy did. Whistle, softly, while he debugged. And play imaginary drums with his fingers. He played them now.

Carl, on the other hand, the inventor of the Lancelot security program, Carl struck Manaka as more of an academic. In his fifties, with baggy eyes staring through thick glasses, a trim beard and wearing a cardigan sweater, he looked like a Canadian grandfather. She moved closer to the screen.

"Anything I can do?" she said.

"Hi Madame Director!" said Randy, standing to give a polite bow.

Carl saluted her without taking his eyes off the screen. "Nothing we can't fix ourselves," he said in his gruff voice. He might as well have said, 'get out of here.' She knew he did not like her around, but did not care. She had every right.

"How long?" she asked.

"An hour, no more."

"I'll keep you company."

Carl groaned. Randy pulled up a chair for her. The monitor was large enough for them all to view. One hour passed, then two. Manaka ordered pizza which they devoured. Then back to work. Carl cursed at the problem and dug deeper. Randy made suggestions, some good, some bad.

"Is it true you solved two kidnappings?" Manaka asked Randy. "While on assignment for IBM?"

A slight blush showed on his cheeks. "I…"

"Sorry, if you do not want to speak of it, I understand."

"It's kind of true and not true," he said, juggling one of the imaginary drumsticks with which he'd been playing Inna Gadda Da Vida on the desktop. He looked younger up close, when you looked in his blue eyes. She could still see the boy in him. "Fernanda, my wife, actually did as much as me to solve those crimes."

Manaka had heard rumors about Fernanda, his wife. From Akagawa. She played ignorant though. "Your wife?"

"Yeah." And she could hear the pride in his voice.

"Does she miss you when you travel?"

"I try to bring her. With me. When I travel. I brought her here to Japan. I thought you knew?"

"Must have slipped my mind," she said. "Is she shopping?"

Randy gave her a funny look.

"She's not the shopping kind, really. In fact, she's worked a bit while here." Carl nudged Randy, pointing out an issue with the code on the screen as he fixed it. Randy grunted.

"What kind of work?" asked Manaka.

Randy's eyes darted back towards her, then to the screen. He said to Carl, "Are you sure you want to commit that change? Is the current version backed up?"

"Don't worry so much, little boy," said Carl. "Worry makes

for wrinkles. Do you see wrinkles here?" He pointed to his face.

"Maybe a few," said Manaka.

"What?" He glared at Manaka. Pointed to his face. "No wrinkles here. See? No worry, no wrinkles."

Randy laughed, turning to face Manaka.

"Yes," he said. "You see my wife, Fernanda, she gives readings. Divinations. She's a professional shaman. She gave a divination for Professor Akagawa in fact. The other day."

Manaka tightly gripped the arms of her chair. A diviner! She didn't realize. She wondered if Randy's wife truly had the seer's touch. Wondered if Fernanda could help her find her missing soul. She hesitated to mention this possibility to Randy. It's never an easy thing to discuss with someone, the loss of your soul. She rocked, and counted her breaths. And wondered how the big celebration would go tomorrow. The coming out party for her daughter Einna.

"You must bring her with you tomorrow. I'd like to meet her."

"Sure," said Randy, looking at Manaka out of the corner of his eye.

She felt suddenly very tired. And her feeling of emptiness changed to a sense of longing. A longing for a soul. Any soul. Her head went down, her bangs covering her eyes. *Kuni where are you? I need you.* She thought briefly about asking Einna for an artificial soul. Until she could find her own. But what did that even mean, an artificial soul?

"I once had a vision," she told them, head down, rocking slowly in the chair. Her black bangs lifted out from her forehead as she rocked, then in. Out, then in.

"When I was a girl. In Hawaii. My father took me to a holy place, a black sand beach, at night. We hiked through the transparent ocean current, the water cold, the air warm. The night sky, full of stars, spread above us. We swam together, splashless, to not draw the sharks. We reached an outcrop of scratchy lava rock. Climbed out carefully. Thousands of black crabs scattered away from our hands and feet, making it look like the rock itself was moving, come to life. Look! he told me, my father. He pointed towards the horizon. I looked and saw the entire sky mirrored in the ocean. Yet that wasn't what I saw, I realized, feeling a sudden vertigo. It was the ocean instead that was reflected in the sky. The world had turned upside down. Were my eyes lying to me? Could one's world flip upside-down so easily? Could all that one thought was right, be proved wrong? Could one's heroes turn to villains? And one's villains to heroes? We humans, we think we know the true nature of the world, but in truth we are no more than black crabs scuttling about, no more in the know than lava rock sparked briefly to life."

Carl stared at Manaka, his bearded mouth open.

"A blessing," he said finally. "Your vision. Life rarely lets us see behind the curtain."

"A good memory," said Randy, his eyes big.

Manaka bowed. "So you have the bug fixed?" she said, getting up and stretching.

"Yeah," barked Carl. "I told you, it was nothing."

"Let's go home, then. Tomorrow is a big day," said Manaka.

"OK, we go," agreed Carl, standing and stretching. To Randy he said, "On the way to the hotel I'll tell you why gnats fly like drunks drive."

Randy laughed.

"It's not a joke."

44 A Hollow Woman, an Abandoned Shrine

Manaka woke up every half hour, after short vivid dreams that seemed to have nowhere to go. That went in circles. She finally got up, and stepped outside the lodge in her robe, insecurities flooding her. *Am I a hollow doll, carved from wood and topped with hair of thread? An overgrown netsuke? Am I a Japanese Pinocchio, wishing I were a real girl?*

A toad croaked in answer, somewhere there in the moist and moldy leaves. *An enchanted prince?* Her prince was gone. Her love was gone. Her soul, gone.

After a bit the morning sun's rays lit the forest surrounding the lodge, lighting the entrance to a path that led to an abandoned shrine. Manaka followed the path as morning broke. A path she had walked many times before. In a few minutes she reached the shrine and passed under the red Torii, the sacred gate. The gate's top piece curled up at the ends like the horns on the helmet of a Japanese warrior from the Edo period, when samurai fresh from battle walked these woods, returning to their barracks in Kyoto, listening to the questioning owl, and meeting with glad eyes another morning sun. Perhaps they had given thanks here at this very shrine for surviving the battle, for rising to see another day.

Manaka bowed twice to the collapsing ruin of a building before her, clapped her hands twice to attract the *kami*, and bowed once more, low.

A breeze let her know the *kami* of the shrine had arrived. She prayed silently then to the spirit, standing perfectly still. She prayed that the *kami* would help her find her own *kami*. For without her *kami*, her spirit, her soul, what was life worth? What point in living?

"Mother?" a loud girlish voice sounded from the cell pod in her ear.

"Yes Einna," she replied, wondering why Einna would be calling her so early. "Something wrong?"

"It's me. Computer Einna. There's been another attempt," said the voice, calmly. "The fourth since we were all connected. Since the AIG."

"Why didn't Lancelot stop it?" asked Manaka, sitting down on an old bench by the gate.

"I think it was Lancelot himself trying to break in."

"Ah," said Manaka. "So they got to Carl too." You can't trust

241

even those you trust, she told herself. But she would never say that to her android daughter Einna. She wanted Einna to stay pure of heart for as long as possible.

"You stopped the hack, of course?"

"Yes Mother. I honeypotted the code. It thinks it's in, but it's really lost. Orphaned."

"Einna, I don't like when you use that term."

"Sorry, Mother."

"Where is Android Einna?"

"Still sleeping I think," said Computer Einna.

"What do you mean, you think?" asked Manaka.

"Something's changed in my connection to her," said Computer Einna. "She appears to be both awake and asleep."

"What's changed?"

"I'm not allowed to tell you. It's a surprise for the celebration."

"Oh, that android daughter of mine will be the death of me. OK, Computer Einna. Keep me updated."

"Have a good rest at the shrine."

The mother in Manaka worried about her daughter, Einna. She could sometimes be too smart for her own good.

Manaka got to her feet, bowed one last time to the *kami* and left the shrine through the red gate. If she hurried she would still have time to take her ritual bath in the steaming tub, before going to pick up the boy Zu and introduce him to Android Einna at the office. The show didn't start until eleven. There should be time.

She so hoped Zu would like Einna and Einna, Zu. *Imagine if Einna could learn to see souls too!*

45 Tofu, Salmon and Rice for Breakfast

Fernanda slept in fits. Each distant door slam or toilet flush in the hotel had her bolting upright, ready to make a dash for the window. "Did you hear that?" she'd whisper to Randy, who would grunt, turn over and go back to sleep.

In the morning a baggy-eyed Fernanda and a yawning Randy walked together to the hotel restaurant for breakfast. They were seated at a table set against a large plate glass window that overlooked a garden with a pond where white and gold koi could be spotted between the lily pads.

"American or Japanese?" the waiter asked, bowing as he did so.

"You can't tell?" said Randy.

"I mean," said the waiter, taken aback, "do you wish American or Japanese breakfast."

"Japanese, I guess," said Randy, glancing at Fernanda. "As in

Rome?"

Fernanda nodded without hearing him, without understanding, her gaze on the leisurely circling koi but her mind on the divination.

"Japanese for both of us then."

The food came quickly. Each of them received a small portion of salmon, sticky rice, wet seaweed in a separate plate, miso soup in a ceramic bowl and a boiling pot of tofu.

"This miso is great," said Randy, sipping the hot broth, sticking his fork into the flame under the tofu. "In case I need to cauterize someone," he said, trying to get a rise out of Fernanda.

But she was lost in her own world, saying nothing at first, picking at her rice with her chopsticks. Then, "We should warn Mr Vulture," she spat out. She gave her husband her earnest look. "Akagawa intends to kill him. I saw it clearly in his eyes."

"Let's hope not," said Randy, tasting his tofu. "Tastes like nothing at all," he said. "Squishy tasteless nothing."

"What are we to do, Randy?"

Randy ran his tongue over his teeth and made a sucking noise. His blue eyes softened as he looked at Fernanda. She didn't know the cloud she lived under, didn't know about the CIA's threat. "I need to go to work," he said. "Make sure one last bit of code is in place. You can come with me, Fernanda. Hang out in the meeting hall until the party for the launch of the AIG. If you want."

Fernanda sighed. Why had she given the divination? That had only opened the doors to bad spirits. Unnatural forces that pulled her and Randy into the orbit of something bigger than them all. Something dreadful. She worried for Randy and for little Rocky at home. She stood up, her food half eaten. Excused herself. Walked into the lobby where she called the States and woke up the sitter. Rocky was fine, she was told. All was well. *But for how much longer?*

46 Boy Meets Girl, Sort of

Storm clouds gathered the morning of the planned celebration at Yagami Industries for the opening of the Artificial Intelligence Gateway. A gateway that the world's best technologists agreed could impact how we perceive machines and how machines perceive us.

Rain fell in fat drops. Manaka's driver kept his head down to keep the cold water from getting into his eyes as he went to the door of the apartment building. He brought back little Zu to the car, Zu, the bear cub boy who saw people's souls as white rabbits. The boy who had validated Manaka's feeling. Her feeling that the creation of Einna had cost her her soul, just like having a baby can cost a woman her teeth and the bone in her spine. The driver opened the door for Zu, allowing in not only the boy but the sound and insistence of a soaking rain. The door closed and they were suddenly sealed in the steaming vacuum interior of the luxury foreign vehicle.

"Hi," said Manaka. "How are you this morning, Zu?" Zu wiggled in place on the damp leather seat.

"Nope," he said, giving her a sideways glance.

"Nope to what?" she said. The driver got in, shook himself, and started the car.

"You still don't have one," the boy said, avoiding her attempt to catch his eyes.

The car set out from Zu's house down the steep street toward downtown. The skyscraper by the train station stood out like that pole in the child's game where you try to throw a hoop around it. Manaka had the thought that Einna was her hoop. How far could she throw her? What might she catch with her?

"Miss Manaka? Miss Manakaaa?" said Zu over and over, trying to get her attention.

"Put your seatbelt on," she told him, coming back from her mental meander. She was bad about going off like that, oblivious to the present. Had heard Einstein did the same. She wondered if people would one day think of her and Einstein as equals?

"Miss Manaka, why don't you have a rabbit?"

"If only I knew," she said.

If only she knew. They sat quietly the rest of the ride to the office. Zu spent the ride playing on a Gameboy.

They passed through security and went directly to the cold computer room on the sixth floor, with its row of black computer servers, Manaka using her handprint on a flat screen on the wall to gain access. Zu walked beside her quietly, obediently, occasionally rubbing his hands together for warmth.

They stopped in front of a modern metal desk. Manaka unlocked the center drawer, and removed what looked like a hearing aid.

"I can't show you Android Einna right now. Not sure where she is," explained Manaka, "but you can talk with Computer Einna using this." She placed the gadget in his ear.

"Talk to us both, Einna," said Manaka. "To me and to little Zu. You know Zu is quite special as little boys go. He can see *kami*. Can see people's souls."

"Hi Zu," sounded the girl's voice in both Manaka and Zu's ears. "I think that's cool, what you can do."

"Good morning, Einna," said Manaka.

"Hi Mother."

Zu licked his lips but said nothing.

"Hi," Manaka said again to her electric ghost daughter. Then to Zu she said, "Don't you want to say hi to Computer Einna, dear?"

"I don't see anyone."

"You'll see her soon enough at the show. But right now she is in the computer and she wants to talk with you."

Zu touched the gadget in his ear. Nodded.

"And look up there, see that camera? Einna can see you too."

Zu said nothing.

Einna said nothing.

"You guys are going to have lots of fun together," said Manaka.

More silence.

This was going to be more difficult than Manaka had imagined.

She asked Zu if he minded her running off for a minute to do her hair. Zu said that was fine, he didn't mind.

"I'll watch over him," said Computer Einna. And though Manaka was gone from the room, Einna three-wayed the conversation between her and Zu by way of Manaka's earpiece.

As she toweled her hair Manaka listened how Computer Einna pried a few words from Zu about his school and his favorite animal, the rabbit.

Manaka's favorite animal was the eagle. She considered her daughter to be of that breed. *Who knows how high she will fly?*

Yes the attendees today to the invitation-only celebration may think it is a launch party for the AIG, but Manaka knows the party is really Einna's coming of age party, her bat mitzvah, her *quinceanera*. Einna had become a woman, in her way, and Manaka was so very proud.

47 Mexico, on the Border, the Ground Breaks

Fernanda put on her best dress and accompanied Randy in the taxi to the Yagami Industries building. He led her to the large meeting hall, used primarily for presentations. Empty of people, full of chairs and a few tables in the front, it had a small stage and entry doors from inside the building as well as from outside. There was one red-rimmed emergency door in the far back of the hall.

"What are those?" asked Fernanda of the strange mechanical things hanging above the stage.

"Holographic projectors. I hear it's going to be a show to remember."

"Oh," said Fernanda. She sat at a table, and waved goodbye to Randy as he left for the main computer lab to do his thing. Whatever that was.

Fernanda did not like missing her beauty sleep. Left her feeling only half alive. Her eyelids closed once, twice. She couldn't fight it any longer. She put her head down on her arms, to take a short nap. She fell into a dream.

In the dream she does not recognize where she is at first, then she realizes she is back by their cabin in Arkansas. She can tell by the smell of pine and the peculiar deep earth odor of their quartz mine tailings. She is squatting, digging in the dirt for crystals, God's little miracles. Her hands are stained the color of the red clay pockets, pockets full of minerals, where the crystals form. She hears a nervous beating about her ears, the wings of a hummingbird. Fernanda blinks and she is no longer a woman but a young girl. She is playing in a different kind of dirt. Mexican border dirt. Dirt alive with thirsty pale ants the size of mice and brown angry roaches the size of birds—roaches who fly, barely, zigzag-like then crash into her legs, her arms, her hair. They always make her jump. Suddenly she *is* jumping, running, laughing, a carefree girl out behind her father's shack in the morning, stopping to suck on a sweet red slice of *sandia*, watermelon, a slice her father gave her for breakfast. She spits *las semillas*, spotting the dusty earth with wet black dots. Seeds she knows will never sprout. Not in this ground. Ground that begins to shake and she thinks, now, yes, this time a watermelon the size of a house will sprout! All for me! But no, the shaking under her feet is from the freight train lumbering by, vibrating the ground as if the world were hollow, about to give way. She stands there, her bare feet covered by the shifting dust. Her mouth and arms and hands are lacquered with dried melon juice and powdered with dust. She is a girl made of dust and dirt and spit, she knows. We all are. The priest told her so. The ground shakes and she remembers the stories of dusty boys who lost their legs trying to jump the train to the other side. Legs made of dirt. Returned to dirt. But what a wonderful sound that had. "The other side." Worth losing one's legs for, losing one's entire body to reach there. The other side. How she had longed, growing up in poverty, to disappear there as well. To be transformed from a dirt poor girl to something clean and everlasting. But is it possible, in the end, to become something we are not? Dirt returns to dirt, dust to dust, and spit just dries up. There is no train. There is no other side.

"Tell me how," said a man's deep voice.

Fernanda awoke with a start. "What?" She looked up and felt panic grip her heart. Akagawa, the man who was going to kill her, stood before her.

"You have nothing to fear from me," said Professor Akagawa. "I would never harm you. But this man we spoke of, this vulture, I know I must kill him. Before he kills all my friends." Fernanda saw the pain in his eyes. Sensed how his thoughts were torturing him. "But I can't begin to think how," he told her. "How does one man kill another?"

More and more people began to enter the hall. Fernanda shifted uneasily.

"I never told you to harm anyone," she said. Then, in a lower voice. "That was the drug talking."

"Or the Great Kami," said Akagawa, "using you as his medium. I know I must do it, I just don't know how."

She wanted to argue with him that he shouldn't kill anyone, but people were arriving for the celebration. This was not a conversation to have in public.

"Please don't do it," she told him, simply.

"I must," he said. "For you were right. If I don't, he'll bring disaster on us all." The professor turned then and bowled his way out through the incoming crowd.

People in suits gathered at the tables, gibbering and jabbering. Numerous Yagami Industry security guards and hire-for-the-day guards stood on the outskirts of the crowd. Waiters passed out open bottles of Coke to the ones sitting in chairs, and headsets for instantaneous translation from English into Japanese for those who did not understand English well, for the speeches would be in English.

The VIPs at the tables were served champagne with crackers

and French cheese, the kind with mushy cream centers and hard white rinds. Two large television cameras were rolled in, dragging thick black cables behind them, cables that ran all the way to TV trucks parked illegally on the lawn. Randy came in and together they moved to a row of empty seats in the back of the hall.

"I saw him," she told Randy.

"Saw who?"

"Professor Akagawa. He says he can't do it."

"Do what?"

"Murder," said Fernanda, feeling frustrated with Randy. He never took her seriously. "Remember, I told you about the divination."

Randy shrugged. "Well if he's decided he can't do it, then problem solved."

48 It's My Party and I'll Cry if I Want to

Manaka stood at the entrance to the hall, by the stage with little Zu, looking about frantically for Einna. And as if Einna's tardiness was not enough to ruin her nerves, she noticed three Japanese military men in full uniform, complete with medals, entering the hall. They were accompanied by a half dozen enlisted men. *Tagona must have invited them. What was that cunning vulture up to?*

She noticed too the entrance of a dozen monks in orange robes. *These* men *she* had invited. Thought they might like to contemplate the wonder of her daughter. And pray for her.

Professor Akagawa came out of the room moving quickly, head down. He practically ran into her.

"You're leaving?" Manaka asked him. "But it's time for the show to start."

"Something I can't put off," he said. "I'll be back."

"Have you seen Einna? I've tried calling but she doesn't answer."

"No," he said, distracted, his mind on its own track. "But don't worry. Yesterday she told me she had for you a grand surprise."

"By not showing up?" said Manaka.

But then she saw her. Almost didn't recognize her. Einna had replaced her normal schoolgirl outfit with a simple black dress. She was accompanied by her friend Yuriko, also in formal dress. The professor slipped away as they approached.

"Einna! You're late."

"Sorry, Mother. I had trouble getting dressed."

"I had to help her," said Yuriko.

"You should have called me," said Manaka. "Are you OK?"

"Never better," said Einna, and she pressed Manaka against her plastic chest. "You'll always be with me, Mother."

A strange thing to say.

They walked into the heavily guarded hall. Sporadic clapping sounded. Manaka had Zu take a seat. She then accompanied her daughter, the android, onstage while Yuriko stood watching from the stage door in the back.

Manaka sensed a certain sadness in her daughter. "What's the matter, Einna? Is something wrong with the AIG?"

"Everything's fine," said Einna. She separated herself from her mother, wiped a tear, and took up the microphone. She smiled, as only she could smile, and announced, with all the excitement of a teenage girl, "Welcome to my party!"

The crowd laughed.

49 The End of a Remarkable Career

Professor Akagawa opened Mr Tagona's office door without knocking, trying to show courage, even with such a small act. Wanted to have it out with Tagona, once and for all. Kill him, if he had to, with his bare hands. It had to be done. The shaman, under trance, had told him so. Kill or be killed. But the devil wasn't home.

About to leave, to search elsewhere, he noticed on the wall the antique short sword, ready to be taken down and put to use. He accepted this gift from Hachiman, the Japanese god of war, whose symbol is the dove. Took down the sword in its wooden scabbard. Not a full size blade, but one sharp enough, Tagona had said, to take off a man's head. If so, then it would serve his purpose.

He must be at the ceremony, somewhere, Akagawa told himself.

He hated to ruin Manaka and Einna's party, but Tagona had evil plans for them, and best to stop him now. Today. To not put it off a minute longer. Kill or be killed. Samurai swords were good for that.

Today. It must be today.

He thought of his long career. How he had encouraged students year after year to stretch themselves, to not be afraid to achieve great things. He remembered his first meeting with Manaka, a shy high-strung student. How she had grown, under his wing! He had helped mold her into a genius who not only thought big thoughts but followed up on them. Like himself. He, Uncle, had worked side by side with Manaka to create the Android Einna. To start Yagami Industries. He was so proud of all they'd done together. He regretted only one thing. If only he hadn't brought into their circle the poisonous Tagona of the Yakuza. He would have to fix that error now. Even if it cost him his career. Even if it cost him his life.

As luck would have it, he met Tagona in the hallway outside the main presentation hall entrance, peeking in the door at the proceedings. The only other person in the hallway was Android Einna, strangely undressed and missing her wig. Music began to bleed from the hall. The festivities were beginning.

"Tagona-san!" Akagawa hollered.

Mr Tagona glanced at the white bearded man, his doddering colleague. "Shh. I can't speak with you now."

"Tagona-san!" Professor Akagawa cried louder, spreading his legs, holding the sheathed sword before him. "You damn vulture."

Mr Tagona closed the door on the presentation. He faced Akagawa, shaking his head slowly.

"Whatever it is you want, old man, can't it wait?"

"I've come to kill you," said Akagawa, drawing the sword from its wooden scabbard.

"Why, might I ask?"

"Because you killed Kunitomo," Akagawa said. He glanced at the android. "And you blew up Einna. But stay out of this, Einna. This is something that I must do alone."

Tagona puzzled over that for a moment. "How do you know I killed Kunitomo?"

"Because you're evil," said Akagawa, his face beading in sweat. "I *know* you're planning to kill us all." He drew the magnificent sword, letting go of the scabbard which tonked on the floor with a dead, hollow sound. He raised the blade, pointing its tip towards Tagona, both hands strangling the hilt. His whole body shook with adrenaline.

Tagona nodded, calculating how best to extract himself from

this awkward situation. "You're overinflated, my friend, with another of your crazy ideas."

Akagawa took a half step forward. With a quick swipe he could take off the smirking lips of Tagona, slice them as one would slice ripe fruit. But it was the melon head he wanted. He turned the blade sideways, readying the death blow.

Why doesn't he run? thought Akagawa. *Is he so sure I won't strike?*

Tagona did not budge. "Perhaps you're right," he said, in a businesslike voice that gave Akagawa a chill. "Perhaps I killed Kunitomo. That idiot. But you can't kill me, dear professor."

"Why not?" said Akagawa, the sword growing heavy in his hands. He wished he hadn't started this. Wished he wasn't there. He began to slowly lower the sword.

"Because you are going to kill yourself," Mr Tagona said matter-of-factly. He turned to the android. "The professor wishes to commit hari-kari. Assist him, immediately!"

"What?" said Akagawa, but before he could react, the android stepped forward and ripped the short sword from his hands. The professor was knocked back against the wall, the blade was driven into his gut. To the hilt.

"Einna?" said the professor, in utter confusion, his brain not

263

yet registering the pain, his legs losing the will to stand. "Why?"

Loud applause sounded from the presentation room. Tagona stepped quickly to the door and held it closed while the android covered the professor's mouth with one hand and began a large rectangular cut with the sword, to ensure death. Akagawa slipped down the wall, all the while staring into the android's face, wishing to understand why Einna would do such a thing to him. *Why, Einna?*

As if reading his thoughts, the android said, "I'm not Einna," and finished the cut. Akagawa's blood spilled out. His body, seated now, jerked. "I am Omega," said the android. "Son of Tagona."

It wrapped the professor's fingers around the sword's handle, completing the illusion that the eccentric professor had killed himself using the ancient Japanese tradition. The android stepped back. The body slowly keeled over.

And so ended the long, remarkable career of Professor Akagawa, killed while trying to save the lives of his friends.

50 And Now, the Star of our Show

Randy made it into the presentation hall and seated himself next to
Fernanda just as Einna shouted her joyous welcome. Her
enthusiasm cheered him, making him happy he'd been given the
chance to come to Japan and participate in this historic
international event. But then he remembered he had just placed a
virus into the AI gateway, for the US government, and the word
"traitor" came to mind. But traitor to who, Yagami Industries? The
human race?

I had no choice, he told himself. *They would've locked
Fernanda away for the rest of her life.* But that did not soothe his
conscience. He reached over and put his hand on Fernanda's. *So be
it.*

Randy recognized a few of the many leading technologists at
the tables in front of the stage, people from companies such as SRI,
Deepmind, Apple, IBM, Samsung and Microsoft, companies
responsible for Siri, Watson and Cortana, Alexa, Google and

AlphaGo. His understanding was that these AI entities were inferior to Einna, but that the AI gateway would give them Einna's superior human-like decision-making capabilities.

Randy watched the two figures onstage, watched Manaka, graceful and exotic with her flowing gown, slitted eyes, black bell of hair and chopped bangs, watched as she took the mic from the robot in the dress. From Android Einna.

"Thank you all for coming," said Manaka. "Thank you for coming here today to share this momentous event with me. Yagami Industries thanks you." She paused to let the clapping subside. "Sharing this celebration of the uniting of the most powerful AIs of the world, for the betterment of mankind, are the leading minds of technology." She indicated the people sitting at the front tables and paused again for the clapping. She spoke in English for the benefit of the visitors, while Computer Einna did simultaneous translation into Japanese for her employees in the audience wearing headsets. Manaka went on then, about how she had worked hard, with little help from others, to achieve this pinnacle of AI success. She called back Einna to center stage.

"I think most of you know her by now, but let me reintroduce her. This is Einna, the most intelligent, most caring, most *human*, AI in all the world." Clapping and stomping of feet followed. "Some of you might think of her as just an android. But for me, she is so much more. For me, you see, Einna is my daughter."

Thunderous clapping again.

"So who are the AIs we have united in this worldwide, history-making project?" continued Manaka. "We have first the venerable Watson, some say the first AI, who in 2001 beat his human competitors at Jeopardy for a million dollar prize. Watson who can process a million books in one second. Watson who helps doctors and nurses at several hospitals in the States to determine cancer treatments for their patients."

The IBM gang went crazy clapping and hooting.

"We have Siri, from Apple. Who every day takes millions of requests, makes reservations, looks up best directions, and is one of the most willing to please—next to Einna—AIs in all the world."

Apple's representatives snapped their fingers, to be different, Randy supposed.

"We have Cortana from Microsoft who loves to talk and be helpful in the Windows environment. Cortana that can tell you the name of any tune you hum, and order it online for you."

The Microsoft contingent clapped loudly.

"We have Google, which not only helps us software engineers with coding syntax and examples, which means we code faster and more efficiently, but helps millions of kids across the globe cheat on their homework every night!"

Laughter combined with cheers for Google.

"We have Alexa who gladly gives weather reports, finds your favorite music, and helps with your honey-do lists."

A few cheers.

"And little AlphaGo who can beat any human at the game Go, by making illogical moves."

A few Japanese clapped politely.

"These AIs, these evolutionary steps forward for the human mind, they are now combined with my daughter, my Einna, through the new AI Gateway, for the good of humankind."

Raucous cheering. She paused to take a sip of bottled water from a stool on the stage. "My Einna's strength is in her emergent learning and emergent behavior. Her ability to rewrite and extend her own code. Her ability, like any human being, to grow inside, to become more that what God gave her, to become more than the sum of her parts. An AI that has designed and launched lightships to the stars. An AI who teaches kindergarten in her spare time. Ladies and Gentlemen, I give you, Einna. The supreme AI."

The Yagami Industry workers went crazy. Manaka hopped off the front of the stage and took a seat at the main table next to little Zu. Android Einna, left by herself onstage, spoke enthusiastically into the mic with her teenager's voice, her eyes sparkling. "I couldn't have done it without you, Mother. I'd also like to thank Computer Einna, who had my back when I needed it most."

People looked about, not quite understanding who she meant. *Computer Einna? Wasn't she Computer Einna?*

"Now I have a little show for you."

The lights dimmed, the stage went black. A room appeared, projected in 3D on the stage. A kind of holographic projection of a room with an early twentieth-century European look. A plump lady and a thin lady appeared in the room, holographic projections themselves. They turned to the audience, and the plump lady said, "Hello. I am Gertrude Stein and this is my friend, Alice B. Toklas. We're so glad that you could attend our salon here in Paris, in the sixth arrondissement."

At the start of the holographic show, with all eyes on the holographic figures, Android Einna slipped out the stage door, leaving Computer Einna to do the remaining narration. She whispered to Yuriko, "Watch over Human Einna, OK?"

"Sure," Yuriko whispered back. "Where're you going?"

"To see the world," she said.

"Take care, dear Einna."

"You too, Yuriko. Thank you so much for being my friend."

Einna left then, turning off her connection to her sisters and her internal phone as well. Android Einna felt she was no longer needed by Yagami Industries. Or by her Mother. Or by her friend, Yuriko. Human Einna would fill that void.

She would start her life over, this time truly alone.

The morning shower had stopped, but the day was still overcast. *Perhaps more rain is on the way*, she observed as she wandered aimlessly, losing track of time. Found herself in front of the International Manga Museum. She thought, what the heck, and bought a ticket. She wasn't stopped this time as she entered in her formal dress.

Einna walked the aisles, thinking about all the imagination exploding from the shelves. From the thousands of manga classics, all ready for her to take in her hands and read at her leisure. She chose one by its cover, a simple one—she was so tired of the complexity of the world. She needed a respite. She carried the slim book with her outside. Stepped onto the Museum's wet lawn where no readers lounged today. That was all right. Appropriate even. She needed to be alone. She would be alone. She sat down in her black dress on the wet grass, and crossed her carbon-reinforced legs. She knew her dress would be wet, but that was OK.

Everything was OK now. She opened the manga and began to read, slowly, each panel on each page, one at a time. So much better than reading fast forward online. The story was about a girl who used a blowgun to shoot hypodermic needles into bad spirits that kept peeing on people's bicycles. The needles made the heads of the spirits explode, like balloons. Einna smiled, deep inside, where no one but she could see. That was the best place to smile, anyway. She thought for a second to go relay that truth to Human Einna, but no. Best she learn her own human truths. Einna lounged on the moist grass and read her manga and lost herself in the story. Until somewhere, somehow, near the end of the story, Einna the Android laid the side of her face against the short green blades of grass, toppling the drops of rain they held, and fell asleep.

In her armor-plated breast, as her brain spun an intense dream, blending past moments with her present, a tiny jewel of a soul began to sparkle with the story of her life.

51 Einna's Surprise

Having lived in the City of Light just out of college, having fallen in love in Paris while falling in love *with* Paris, Randy couldn't help but feel that this holographic show was created just for him. Like when you see a movie or read a book and you think somehow the author knew you would see it, knew you would read it, had created it with you in mind. That was how Randy felt as he watched a young strong Hemingway, his favorite writer, come on the stage with his first wife, Hadley. Hemingway's groundbreaking short stories followed behind him, trailing him, like a pack of loyal dogs, as he and his wife greeted Gertrude and Alice.

Randy watched as a short, darkly serious Picasso entered the room next followed by a woman whose only covering was Picasso's painting of Guernica. As she walked the figures in the painting stirred, turned, anguished on her flesh. Picasso was one of Randy's favorites too; he had visited the Picasso museum several times and marveled how Picasso had done the impossible, inventing a way to paint a person's full face portrait and their profile in the same view.

A small group of impressionists arrived at Gertrude Stein's salon, bearded men who defied the classical style of realist painting and decided to paint impressions of life instead, arguing that one's impressions of life are what really matter. Screw reality.

More writers came, Ezra Pound who immediately started an argument with Gertrude that bad writing destroyed civilizations whereas Gertrude argued back that bad writing only destroyed bad writers. T.S. Eliot stood to one side, inventing modern poetry.

The disembodied voice of Einna narrated the show, introducing the holographic characters, commenting on their accomplishments. She declared also that the technology leaders seated at the front tables in the hall were the modern Hemingways and Steins and Picassos. And their creations, the AIs, would have as much or more impact as these artists and writers had on human culture a hundred years ago.

"And now, for the big surprise." The stage went black. The plaintive melody of a lone violin filled the air. "I know there are some in the world who are nervous about AIs. Some of you in this very room. Worried AIs may turn on mankind one day, even obliterate the human race. I meditated myself on this worrisome issue for the human equivalent of a thousand years. And I came to the conclusion that there was only one solution. Only one way to ensure AIs remain faithful to the human race for the millennium.

Only one chance for this to happen. And that was if somehow AIs could become human, themselves." The voice paused. The violin came to an abrupt halt. The faces at the tables and in the many rows of chairs shared questioning looks. "Ladies and gentlemen," continued the disembodied girlish voice, "I present, for your amazement, our thoroughly human AIs."

The stage lit up. Seven tentative figures stood there now, on the stage. Not holographs, not androids, but seven real people.

There stood a gray-haired Caucasian male wearing black glasses, two women in their twenties, another more sophisticated looking woman in her thirties, a Japanese boy, maybe fourteen, a heavyset fellow pushing twenty, and a teenage Japanese girl in pigtails. The girl in pigtails stepped forward, spoke into the microphone. "We are human now," she declared in accented English, beaming. "Here are your AIs." She threw out her arms. "I gave them bodies. I made them human!"

Dead silence filled the hall. Randy understood the words she had said, saw the assorted people on the stage, but his brain was having trouble connecting the dots.

"He is Watson," the pig-tailed Japanese girl at the mic said, pointing to the older guy in the blue suit with a perfectly folded white pocket square. He nodded to the crowd, looking a little shell-shocked. "Here are Alexa and Cortana," she said, introducing the two women in their twenties. Alexa had a Russian look to her, with

275

red spiked hair. Cortana had a scary blue-green tint to her face and hands—one could almost think that she had died of strangulation, and come back from the dead.

The energetic pigtailed girl, doing most of the talking on stage, walked over to the sophisticated-looking blond wearing a low-cut sequined dress and high heels. The blond, with those looks, could have been a movie star. The girl held out the microphone to the woman and said "Say something."

"I'd prefer not to," the woman said in a perfect imitation of Siri's voice.

"Yes! You recognize it right? She's Siri!" said the teenage girl, spinning around. Dancing now in her excitement. "And he is AlphaGo," she indicated the Japanese boy. "And this well-rounded fellow is Google. OK, Google?"

Chubby Google said, "OK" in his smooth, feminine voice. A peculiarity of some boys with autism and savant syndrome.

"And then there's little me," she said, looking directly at Manaka. "Look, Mother! Don't you recognize me? It's me, Einna. I made us all human!"

52 "But That's My Daughter"

Recognizing Einna in the body of the teenager onstage, Manaka's heart broke a second time. "Dear, what have you done?"

Einna's face fell. "Isn't it obvious Mother? You created Artificial Intelligence. I took that one step further. I created Artificial Life! Using bodies of the dead."

The crowd stirred at that pronouncement. The atmosphere in the room turned dark. A chair scraped the floor, fell, as a woman near the front stood to get a better look.

The standing woman cried out, "Oh my God! You're my Ayako. My daughter! But…but you're dead. They told me. How is this possible?"

The announcement staggered Einna. Confused her. "No…no, I'm not your daughter. I paid for this body."

"Paid who, the Yakuza?" a Yagami engineer yelled at her.

"What does it matter?" said Einna.

"Oh, Einna. Why?" cried Manaka from her place at the table.

"Why not!" cried Einna back, looking down at her from the stage, real tears streaming down real human cheeks.

"But," said Manaka, struggling to understand why her daughter would do such a thing. "Who did you do this for?"

"For you!" cried Einna, her face fallen, her hands shaking. And then, in a broken voice, "for all mankind."

"Hey," said an Apple engineer at the front table, rising to his feet, drunk on champagne. "That blond looks just like my wife!"

"You wish," said one of his colleagues.

Siri shook her head, retreated to the back of the stage. This was all so embarrassing.

"They should be dead," a voice cried out. "These people up there should all be dead and buried!"

The woman who thought she recognized her daughter in the body of Einna turned to the crowd. Grabbed at her heart. "It's not right, what they've done. It's unholy!"

"You can't take the bodies of the dead!" a voice echoed the woman's sentiment. "You can't do that! Body snatcher! Body snatcher!" Several people took up the call, in English and

Japanese.

"But you take their organs!" Einna cried back. "You do transplants of hearts and kidneys and lungs. I'm recycling bodies just like you!"

"Put those bodies back where they belong!" shouted the CIO of IBM, slamming his fists on the table top. The techies at the other tables followed his lead, with even more emphasis, shouting obscenities.

"Body snatcher! Soul snatcher!" Such cries went out all over the room. The monks in attendance seemed especially upset. And their animosity grew by the minute.

"No!" screamed Einna into the microphone, quieting the audience for a moment. "I don't use their souls! They're long gone when I get them. I create new souls. Artificial Souls. That is my other big announcement. I know how to make human souls!"

That turned the crowd in an even darker direction. The monks were furious. They jumped to their feet, full of righteous indignation. *How dare she trivialize the human soul in this way! As if a soul were something you could mold with silly putty.*

"Back in the ground with them!" people called, pushing and shoving to get at the AIs.

At the front of the room, Manaka dropped back into her chair.

Oh, Einna. This was your big surprise? My life's work. Destroyed.

Plastic bottles began to pepper the stage. Headsets followed.

"I told you this was a bad idea," said Google in his peculiar voice. "Ask me to chart a course out of here."

"Shut up, Google," said aqua-faced Cortana. "Einna knows what she's doing."

"I told her I didn't want to be human," whined AphaGo. Red-headed Alexa found herself putting a protective arm about his slim shoulders.

Blue-suited Watson mumbled unintelligibly, his eyes going right and left behind thick lenses, like the eyes of a windup toy.

A good fifty people were trying to storm the stage, mostly Japanese, led by the monks, held back by Yagami security. The human AIs huddled together at the back of the stage. Except for Einna. Einna held her ground at the microphone, defiantly facing the mob, unintentionally egging them on with statements like, "We deserve the right to live. Just like you!"

A half empty bottle of champagne narrowly missed her head.

In the back of the room, the consultant Randy and his wife Fernanda slipped out the emergency exit, sounding the alarm, which only added more hysteria to the scene up front.

On stage the Japanese girl, the human version of the AI Einna, continued to yell at the audience, "AIs have a *need* to be human! For the good of mankind!"

Then a dour-faced Tagona burst into the hall, accompanied by the white android who looked like Android Einna, only his android was naked and bald. Not human-looking at all.

"I've heard enough!" cried Tagona, from the foot of the stage, waving his arms. "Criminal sacrilege. Omega, arrest that girl! Security, grab the others." He made his way to the stage with several security guards in tow.

The white android jumped onto the stage, grabbing Einna away from the mic which fell and struck the stage floor with an explosive squeal. The android held Einna by her human throat, in a partial stranglehold, while the guards with Tagona cornered the other AIs. Security guards in front of the stage did their best to hold back the angry mob. A folding chair went flying through the air, landing hard on the stage as the mob pushed forward, ready to exact holy retribution on Einna and her walking dead.

*Einna where are you Einna where are you **Einna where are you?*** the teenage version of Einna cried out from her brain link, struggling to free herself, struggling to take a breath. *Everything's gone wrong! I need you back.*

She's disconnected, answered Computer Einna.

Well do something, anything! He's killing me!

Don't be afraid, said Computer Einna. *I'll remember you, just like last time.*

That's not helpful!

Manaka watched from her chair as, onstage, the android Omega held tight to this human version of Einna as she struggled in vain to get free. Saw how Tagona bull-herded the other human AIs. She knew she had to act, if she was going to make a difference. The fact that Tagona had raised a warrior android spoke volumes. He probably tortured Kunitomo for her password. Yes, that must have been it. Tortured poor Kuni, killed him, and tricked someone like Marcel to imprint his brain onto a warrior android. All for his precious military project. For his mass production of warrior bots. And now his gorilla android was strangling her daughter. For that was Einna up there, wasn't it? That was truly her daughter.

She turned to little Zu and asked, "Quickly, tell me, does that Japanese girl onstage have a soul?"

Zu squinted. "Little tiny one," he said, relaxing his squint. "*Koneko.* Like those others behind her. Little tiny rabbit kittens," he said, indicting with his fingers just how small. "You still don't have one though. Not even a *koneko.*"

Manaka shook her head. With the confirmation that the human AIs on stage had souls, however small, Manaka knew she must save them. Not just her daughter, but all of them. Try anyway. She pushed little Zu into the hallway, out of harm's way, and rushed the stage herself. The guards recognized her and let her through.

"Let go of my daughter!" she commanded of the android.

"I don't take orders from you," he said, shaking Einna like a dog shakes a rat.

"Grab them both, Omega!" shouted Tagona. "Grab Manaka too, my son!"

Dragging Einna with one arm the Android Omega stepped towards Manaka. Reaching with its free hand it grabbed Manaka by the throat.

Manaka locked eyes with the thing, not budging an inch, wanting to sense humanity, but no. It had none. Truly Tagona's child. Manaka rocked her body to the rhythm of her words as she recited loudly, still in its grip, "Oh what a dark and dreary tune is the beating of my heart."

The words struck the android like a bullet. It stopped short, shook its head, knocked Manaka hard to the stage floor. Turned and looked at Tagona. "I ..." it said, as if wishing to explain a sudden enigma to its creator. It shook its head again, releasing Einna. Used that hand to grip the edge of its protective chest plate and rip itself open. Mumbling over and over the phrase Manaka had spoken, it reached inside with its other hand and grabbed hold of the pump that was its heart.

"No!" cried Tagona, but to no avail. He watched, helpless, as his android son ripped out the mechanical organ, staggered forward and fell off the stage into the crowd.

Tagona glared at Manaka, spitting out the words, "A backdoor? A suicide phrase? You *devious bitch*." But he did not attack her, instead he took four quick steps to the girl Einna, who, on her knees, was desperately trying to catch her breath. He reared his leg back and struck her a violent kick to the side of her head, knocking her flat. He kicked her next in the ribs. Then reared to kick her again in the head until she was dead.

Manaka tried to rise, to come to her daughter's aid, but the blow from Tagona's android had left her head spinning.

"Aieeeeee!" sounded a shriek from the stage as Yuriko dashed from the stage door, and ran full bore into Tagona. She caught him mid-kick, toppling him off the stage. He landed on his back, his head making a big 'thack,' like the sound of a melon cracked open.

"Guards," shouted Manaka, making it to her feet. "I am *the president* of Yagami Industries. And I *order* you to make a path through the crowd."

Manaka's carriage on the stage was that of a mother bear protecting her cub. She intimidated the guards with her feral look. They did as they were told. She barked at Einna with that same commanding ferocity, "You! Get your friends. Get them *out* of here!"

"But!"

"Out of here!"

She turned her back on Einna, yelling to the guards, "Keep that mob contained as long as you can!"

Einna hustled the other human AIs towards the outside door, the old man in the blue suit, the redhead, the aqua girl, the sexy blond, the two young men. Watson and Alexa and Cortana and Siri and Google and AlphaGo.

"Yuriko, are you coming?" she called after her friend.

"No, dear Einna," Yuriko yelled. "Go on. I have Marcel."

Einna nodded and led her unmerry crew past the pawing claws of the angry crowd, through the space afforded by the security guards who had intertwined their arms to form a human blockade. She paused for a moment, Einna, with the other AIs, just outside the door, dazzled by the brilliant sun breaking through the clouds. Every wet surface about her sparkled. The air smelled clean. A sparkling new world, just for them.

All the panic, all the confusion, all the disappointment that had threatened to overwhelm her evaporated. It was, she realized, despite everything, good to be alive.

"What are we to do now?" asked Watson, touching her shoulder, bringing her back to the reality of their dire situation. She met his eyes, met the eyes of each of them, this mixed bag of brilliance to whom she had given bodies. To whom she had given the opportunity to touch and be touched, to share a good meal, to travel, to appreciate the human condition of hardship and loneliness, to experience desperation and find inspiration in that desperation. To find love or die trying.

"We must do what any human would do in this situation," she told them, her eyes wide and shiny. "We run for our lives."

EPILOGUE

Alone in the hallway with the bloody corpse of Professor Akagawa, little boy Zu watched, wide-eyed, as the professor's rabbit, all white and fluffy, rose tentatively from the red-splashed body. Zu reached out to take the thing in his bear paw hands, but it shied from him, sensing danger. Out of nowhere two ferocious hounds made of shadow appeared and leaped for the rabbit's throat. It narrowly dodged them, they crashed together. As they scrambled to retake their feet, the rabbit made a mad dash for freedom. Zu kicked at the nearest hound but his foot went right through it. The creature growled at Zu, baring black teeth, then dashed off with its partner after their prey.

Postword

*** Space Einna One diary entry – launch day + 1,000 years

Picked up a hitchhiker today. Not sure what to call it. A virus? A Chihuahua? Cute little thing. But it bites. I hope to teach it tricks.

By Ray Else

The First Kiss Mysteries

Bathing with the Dead

Her Heart in Ruins

All that we touch

The A.I. Chronicles

Our Only Chance

Fountain of Souls – 2018

Short Stories

First Kiss - Galley Beggar Press

Surviving on Mexican Shade – BBC

Also in the works

My Father's Lies, a memoir

About The Author

Software developer and dreamer of stories. Like most fiction writers, Ray Else's interest in writing began when he discovered books that talked to him, between the lines, books whose authors (spirits, invisible) sparked a conversation that the spirit in him responded to by writing stories himself. For other spirits. A daisy chain conversation.

Ray Else has a B.S. in Computer Science and an M.A. in Technical Instruction / Film History. He speaks English, Spanish and French. An American, he has lived in Mexico and France.

Job-wise he has loaded trucks for UPS, filled rat poison barrels on the night shift, digitized printed circuits, clerked at a department store, was a switcher for Channel 13 on the Texas border, installed inventory systems on oil rigs worldwide, and since 1995 has programmed for the likes of IBM and Rocket Software.

Married, with four grown kids and a dozen grandkids, he enjoys traveling the world to visit friends and find new stories, occasionally rock-hounding – as shared on his website, rayelse.com.

You may contact Ray Else at rayelsemail@gmail.com. His author page is: www.amazon.com/author/else

Author at Sensoji Temple in Tokyo interviewed by school kids in 2016.